"Robert White's 'Silent W... ...to unfamiliar territory. It has strong story line told from a viewpoint distant from that of the usual mystery novel. Once begun, I wanted to know where it would take me...to the end."

–**Gale Cook, Retired Reporter**
Major San Francisco Newspaper

"A gripping book from cover to cover. The author exquisitely captivates with a fast paced, spellbinding story of courage, psychological intrigue...and murder.

–**James J. Whelan, Ph.D.**
Clinical Psychologist

"Bob White's hard-hitting first novel paints a realistic picture of the courts, juvenile justice system and law enforcement. With a terse writing style reminiscent of Raymond Chandler, White brings to life a new and exciting detective hero--a social worker who bucks the odds to seek justice for a young man in his caseload."

–**Art German,**
Sacramento Bee Columnist

"Bob White's 'Silent Witness' was a great and enjoyable read. Loved the protagonist and would like to see him in a movie or TV series."

–**Mehl Simmons, Past President,**
California Chapter,
National Association of Social Workers

"A clever weaving of murder and suspense with the rigors of modern-day social work. Would that every juvenile had as dedicated an adult advocating on his/her behalf.

"As owners of a bookstore, we are certainly grateful for Bob White's contribution to what I'm sure will be recognized as popular literature. It was our pleasure to be among the first to read 'Silent Witness.'"

—Jim Crawford,
Owner, Crawford's Books

"If you are tired of the same old hard nosed, gun toting, wisecracking private eye or ex-cop stereotype solving the puzzle, you will enjoy 'Silent Witness' by Robert White.

"When a street-wise juvenile delinquent accused of murdering his adoptive father is jailed for the crime, Jay Kenderson, his social worker/probation officer refuses to abandon the boy resulting in his risking his life and his family's when he finds himself enmeshed with corrupt police and politicians.

"White is an author who writes about what he knows, using his expertise as a career social worker to create his everyday hero and giving us an insight into a world of teenage offenders."

–Nan Mahon,
Elk Grove Citizen

"As Kenderson works to prove the innocence of his young client, he finds himself embroiled in a dangerous world where death is the likely price to be paid for bringing the truth to light. As a counselor and client share a series of frighteningly close brushes with danger, the youth gradually begins to drop his defenses and fearfully dares to experiment with trusting another human being."

–Darla Welles,
Porterville Recorder

For Guy and the two Fredas,
Jack and Dorothy,
Thelma and Garry
who are with us in memory;
and to the rest of my extended family who are still here.

And to my wife Sue, who has performed a host of services in the
production of this book, heartfelt thanks.

Robert White, a native Californian, is a Licensed Clinical Social Worker now retired from a career in both youth corrections and outpatient treatment of emotionally stressed clients. Still working with a small private practice, he is currently director of a support group for parents of teens at risk and working on a second mystery novel.

Library of Congress Catalog Card Number: 97-090894

ISBN 0-9659865-0-0

Printed in the United States of America

SILENT WITNESS

Robert White

Dunlop-Wade Publishers

In Celebration of the Centennial of Social Work,
This Book is Dedicated to
Social Workers Past and Present,
Who Have Never Stopped Giving, Caring and Helping.

SUNDAY LATE AFTERNOON

Feeling strangely uneasy, he moved to the kitchen, lifting the wall phone. A man's impatient voice asked for James Kenderson.

"I'm Kenderson."

"This is Detective Al Fallon, Santa Inglesia police. We're trying to locate Freddie Hawkins. Do you know where he is?"

Kenderson frowned. "What's he done now?"

"You're his probation officer or social worker, right?"

"Yes."

"You supervise the special diversion program for sons of rich kids, right?"

Kenderson's face grew hot. "No, that's not right. Money hasn't anything to do with who's assigned."

"Right." The detective's voice dripped doubt.

"So what's happened? Why are you looking for Freddie?"

"His stepdad, I guess it's his adoptive father, was killed."

Kenderson's stomach tightened. "What happened?"

After a delay, Fallon said, "The old man's head was bashed in with a statuette.

Kenderson felt like he'd been whanged with a ball bat. If Freddie was guilty, an adult court would commit him to the California Youth Authority. After his twenty-fifth birthday, hard time in a state prison would begin. Kenderson feared the notoriety would end the diversion project and his prized casework position.

Fallon's brusque "hello?" snapped his gloomy thoughts and Kenderson quickly replied, "I'll start looking for him."

Detective Fallon grunted as Kenderson cradled the phone.

"What was that about?" asked Fran, his pretty, brunette wife as she walked into the kitchen.

"Earl Hawkins was murdered! The police want to talk to Freddie. I've got to find him."

"They think he did it?"

"I'm sure they do. He's bragged for years he was going to kill the man. God knows what he'll say if they pick him up."

It had been an unusually quiet afternoon until that shattering moment. James Kenderson, Jay, to his friends, had secretly feared Freddie would someday explode into violence. He'd been half-watching the final minutes of the San Francisco Forty-Niner, Oakland Raiders exhibition football game expecting phone calls from his wards that began, "Can I do this, Mr. Kenderson?" There were only fifteen boys on his Diversion Center caseload, ninety to a hundred was the normal number, but his relationship with each had developed over the months into something between a cop and a big brother. Frantic parents often phoned, wanting to know what to do about truancy, drugs, gang affiliations, disrespect. The list went on and on. Normally, and to the great annoyance of Fran, the family had few peaceful nights or weekends since he'd accepted the Social Work position with the experimental project.

"Honey, it's the price of being assigned to a high visibility prevention program." They designed the Center, funded through the Federal Office of Juvenile Justice, to demonstrate that Status Offenders, truants, runaways and beyond-parental-control youth, could be kept out of the Oso County Juvenile Hall and Santa Inglesia's jail, if closely supervised by a professional social worker. Thanks to his holding a Clinical Social Work License, and his Youth Authority experience, Kenderson, two days after his forty-sixth birthday, landed the job in California's San Joaquin Valley's second largest city.

On this last day of August, it was too warm for a sweater. Picking up his wallet and the keys to Fran's Plymouth, he started out the door. "I need your car. Think I know where he'll be." Fran sighed as he hurried out the front door. She walked back to the office/den and continued working at the computer on her golf group rosters.

Heading toward the Meadows, Santa Inglesia's ghetto, bounded by the Oso River on the west and Fifth Street on the east, James Kenderson, six-feet-one and possessor of a full head of slightly graying auburn hair, thought about his own kids. Fifteen-year-old Cindy was out with her new boyfriend. Vernon, his sixteen and a half year old, had nagged him into letting him use the latter's 1972 Datsun that he'd lovingly purchased after years of reconstructive surgery on a shattered right knee, compliments of his short medic tour in Viet Nam. The brown Datsun's odometer read 245,635 miles and was the object of friendly derision. However, its purchase had marked the beginning of his long-delayed postwar life and he had no intention of parting with it.

Kenderson had objected to Freddie Hawkins being assigned to his caseload because they had ignored the sixteen year old's extensive rap sheet with the police. His adoptive father's political influence that had shielded his son from the consequences of his actions, had also assured the boy's inclusion in the special project. It was galling, being forced to accept this out-of-control boy whom they had recently diagnosed Attention Deficit Hyperactive Disorder. He'd reviewed his Diagnostic Manual which reported that such individuals suffer from inattention, hyperactivity and impulsivity. After one contact with Freddie Hawkins, Kenderson understood why adults who dealt with such youngsters wished they had pursued other careers.

Fran, who job-shared three mornings a week at the District Attorney's Office, and his psychologist intern friend, Nehemiah Hayes, "Nehi," shared a common view. Nehi put it simply, "Freddie'll have you begging Nate Farber, your upward-striving boss, for mercy, which he won't give because you don't kiss his ass."

Driving quickly through light traffic, Kenderson parked in front of a grimy, one story concrete block building with several letters missing from the Bar and Grill sign above the door. A short, dark man hurried out the door. He recognized Rico Jones, a pimp Freddie hung out with. Hustling out of the Plymouth, he called, "Hey Rico, have you seen Freddie?"

The dark-skinned man cringed but, after recognizing Kenderson, relaxed. "He and the fat kid he hangs around with just split."

"How long ago?"

"About ten minutes." Rico looked nervous. "Why you want him?"

Kenderson weighed not telling Rico about the crime, but decided everyone in the state of California would learn about the murder before the night was over.

"Earl Hawkins was killed tonight. Freddie's a suspect."

To Kenderson's surprise, the small man suddenly fled down the street mumbling, "Oh shit, Arnie Setich."

Kenderson drove slowly south on Third Street toward Santa Inglesia's riverside business district, scanning both sides of the street. Three blocks later, he recognized Freddie and his friend, Ermon. Kenderson steered to the curb ahead of them and stepped out. Freddie, small for his age and blond, looked like he was about to run.

"Freddie, the police are looking for you. Get in the car and I'll take you home."

The boy glared. "No way. Me and Ermon here are looking for big time hookers to hit on for money."

Kenderson weighed how best to tell Freddie what had happened, then decided there was no best way. "Freddie, your dad's been killed."

It took the boy a long moment before he reacted. "You're kidding me. Somebody finally put a bullet in his head." He began to laugh and pounded Ermon on the back. "You hear that man! Super news! We can live like kings."

Kenderson moved closer and took the boys arm. "Freddie, the police think you killed him."

Freddie wasn't fazed. "I should'a done it a long time ago Who do I send a barrel of champagne to?"

"They think you killed him." Kenderson persisted. He realized he was talking to thin air. Freddie was absorbed in daydreams of wealth and freedom. He took Freddie's arm again. "Please get in or the next ride will be in a black and white."

Freddie gave that thought two seconds and was about to dismiss it, when Ermon spoke. "Better go, Freddie, you don't want nobody fucking with your money, right?"

Freddie grinned. "Cool. Later."

He climbed into Kenderson's car without another word and on the way home, bounced in the seat, exulting aloud about his new found bonanza. The Hawkins family was a strange mixture, Kenderson reflected. He'd met them all in the course

of working almost daily with Freddie the past two months. Earl
Hawkins' youngest son, Phillip, an attorney and Assemblyman,
was running for the State Senate in the fall. He and his father
were a mutual admiration society, as one observer put it. Pete,
the dark, hulking, eldest, in contrast, served as a gofer to his
father and his father's hard-nosed assistant, Arnie Setich. Then
there was Freddie. His adoptive mother, the former Clarissa
MacCormick, according to police reports, had   committed
suicide less than a year ago. And finally, the recently deceased
patriarch, revered by Santa Inglesians as a saint who supported
progressive causes with money and influence, had been the king
maker of Santa Inglesia and Oso County for many years.

Kenderson hoped the sight of the body would bring the
boy back to earth. "Freddie, be careful what you say. Think
before you talk. Remember the times we've gone over that,
okay?"

Freddie pretended to agree. Kenderson wondered if he
should take more time to prepare the boy for what was coming.
He instantly abandoned the idea because the ADHD youth had
taught him that no matter how much they rehearsed, especially
before court appearances, Freddie marched to his own heedless,
hyperactive drummer.

Hilltop Terrace was crowded with logoed, antenna-
sprouting TV trucks. Kenderson parked down the street and led
Freddie through the babble and under the yellow tape barrier as
inconspicuously as he could, but pandemonium broke loose
when a reporter from the *Sentinel* spotted Freddie. A police
officer stopped them. Kenderson flashed his probation shield
and had to shout to be heard. The officer waved them along. As
they entered the heavy oak front door, Kenderson said:
"Freddie, just tell the truth and you'll be all right."

Sergeant Raul Castro, a wiry, intense Hispanic, whose detectives called Bulldog, looked down at Earl Hawkins' six-foot four-inch, 275-pound body, face down on the thick rug. Drying blood matted sections of his skull, which had apparently received repeated blows from the heavy, bronze statuette of a football player lying next to him. No question the heavy, blood-caked, trophy was the murder weapon. It looked like an impulse killing. He envisioned a quarrel preceding the attack. The victim had been sitting, and his assailant was undoubtedly someone Earl Hawkins knew. Castro recalled that Hawkins was a powerful man who worked out in the Valley Athletic Club. There was no evidence he'd struggled with his attacker.

The dim interior of the huge vault-ceilinged room, lined with book shelves, made Castro feel like he was in a public library. Scattered deeds and escrow papers covered the desk, mute evidence Hawkins' prosperous real estate business had been conducted from this room. A top of the line computer sat on the side opposite an overturned pedestal. The Sergeant had noted the teakwood stand where, he guessed, the statuette normally rested. He motioned to Fallon. "Any word on the kid?"

Fallon shook his head. "I phoned his social worker, a guy named Kenderson. He said he'd start looking for him. It was bound to happen. The kid's a loose cannon. I understand he's been picked up twenty, thirty times over the years." Castro nodded, absently.

The forensic team arrived. Cameras flashed and tape measurements were jotted in notebooks. Ed Forsythe, longtime Medical Examiner of Oso County, knelt beside the victim. "How long has he been dead?" Castro asked.

"The body temperature loss is minimal but other signs, like lividity, are a little puzzling. It's a cool seventy degrees in here according to the thermostat, but his body temp is around ninety-six."

"So, doc, give me an estimate, okay?"

"I did a temp two inches down his esophagus, plus a rectal. On average, I'm guessing two to two and a half hours."

"Four to four-thirty?"

"Right, unless we find something during autopsy."

"Who called it in?"

"The live-in housekeeper, a Mrs. Nabors, a little after six thirty. She was just coming back from visiting her sister, who lives on a farm west of here. She has her own key."

"Where is she now?"

"Phoned her sister to come get her. I'll talk to her in the morning after she's calmed down."

Castro grimaced, hearing the horde of reporters and TV anchors baying at the door. He'd given orders to keep them outside the taped area surrounding the mansion.

A heavyset detective Lieutenant, Fred Coughlan, in tight pants and shirt, approached Castro, carefully skirting the chalk outline around the body and the blood stains near the statue. "My God, who would have dared off the main man?"

Castro looked up to see a badly shaken Lieutenant practically wringing his hands. "He wasn't my squad's main man." Castro couldn't resist the shot. Cops not on the take, knew Coughlan and his superiors were paid to protect Hawkins' Meadows operation from complaining merchants, who either paid up or were beat up. Arnie Setich did the enforcing.

Coughlan asked, "His kid did it? Looks like Hawkins knew his assailant. There's no sign of a struggle. Maybe there was a big argument, then this."

"Could be. We're looking for the boy now."

Jim Cunningham, a slim, bespectacled medical technician, looked up from his laptop computer and called out.

"Raul, we compared the prints on the statuette with Freddie Hawkins' prints we had on file. They match."

Sergeant Castro spotted Kenderson and Freddie the moment they walked through the library door and beckoned them over. Kenderson took in the scene. The body had not been removed and he waited for Freddie's reaction. There was a look of momentary shock on the boy's face but it disappeared when, grinning, he moved closer to the crumpled body.

Lieutenant Castro looked unhappy. Dealing with a juvenile homicide suspect was a pain in the ass. Phone the DA's office, wait till they run down some deputy DA, and then get some half-baked response that was no help? To hell with it. He pulled out his Miranda Rights card and began to read. He should have known. The boy hardly listened. "I don't need no lawyer. They're all crooks anyway."

Castro turned to Kenderson. "Any objections my asking him questions? Maybe we can clear this up quick." Kenderson shook his head. It wasn't the questions that worried him, it would be Freddie's answers.

Castro began, "Did you kill your father?"

Kenderson held his breath, hoping Freddie wouldn't destroy himself, but that was not to be. Smirking, he told Castro: "That fucker was not my father. I don't know who my real father was."

The detective flushed. "I'll have to place you under arrest if you don't give me straight answers." Freddie said, "Fuck you." Castro turned to Fallon. "Have a couple of uniforms take him downtown and book him." Kenderson expected Freddie to run, but a compact-looking guy with short, brown hair he guessed was Fallon, pinioned the boy's wrists and with help from a uniform, slid on handcuffs.

Castro looked at Kenderson. "Do you know how to reach his brothers? They'll want to notify the family attorney."

Kenderson shook his head. "He's a juvenile. He doesn't need an attorney now. He should be placed in Juvenile Hall."

"Come on, you know he'll be tried as an adult. At his age, every judge in this county will remand a murdering juvenile to adult court."

Kenderson bristled. "He's not a murdering juvenile until he's convicted."

Watching Castro's reaction, Kenderson realized he wasn't doing Freddie or himself any good. "Could I talk to you a minute in private?" Castro nodded to Fallon, who joined him. They led the way to a corner of the library. Kenderson was on the verge of warning Castro it was illegal to lock up a minor with adults. He didn't bother knowing most judges would sanction a more secure setting for older teenagers accused of a capital crime. Since Freddie had broken out of juvenile hall several times in the past, he knew any appeal would fall on deaf ears.

Once out of earshot, Kenderson said: "When I told Freddie his father had been killed, he thought it was a gunshot. The boy is his own worst enemy. He has this attention deficit disorder which makes him unpredictable but not violent. Ritalin makes him quieter and more rational, but often he won't take it."

Castro shook his head. "Those are matters for the experts and the courts. For now, I consider him our prime suspect. His fingerprints are all over that statuette and he's well known for his explosive temper." Fallon sneered, "Want to let the poor, little, rich kid go? You social work types are all alike. We catch the bastards and you beg the judge to let'em go because they had bad parents."

Kenderson felt his face flush. He was grateful when Castro turned to Fallon and said, "Cool it."

Castro walked away but Kenderson caught up to him. "What if Freddie has an alibi? Maybe Ermon can tell us where he was at the time of the killing."

Castro raised his hands. "One crazy kid is going to alibi another? Give me a break."

"When does the medical examiner think he was killed?"

Castro shrugged. "A ball park estimate. Sometime after four o'clock. Probably no earlier."

Kenderson persisted. "How is the time determined?"

Castro's impatience showed. "Body temperature, mostly. The ME said the body was still warm, about 96 degrees."

"Thanks."

Freddie, with his hands cuffed behind his back, was yelling "faggots" at the two officers who stood alongside. Kenderson moved in close. "Freddie, when did you and Ermon get together today?"

Freddie shrugged his shoulders and began mouthing off again. Kenderson raised his voice. "Think, man, think! When?"

He tried to ignore his caseworker, but Kenderson persisted. "Okay, man, around three-thirty. You satisfied?"

"You're sure?"

"Man, I said it didn't I? Ask Ermon, okay?"

Two uniforms marched Freddie off between them. Kenderson walked alongside the boy. "I'll come see you as soon as I can." Freddie, still yelling, didn't turn around as he was eased into the back seat of the police car.

Kenderson returned to the library where the forensic team was still busy. He approached Castro and Fallon. "Sergeant, Freddie's wild and unpredictable but I don't think he's capable of murder. Something in his makeup stops him before he goes too far. I've seen it happen several times."

Robert White

Fallon laughed, "You don't call driving down a main traffic street at sixty plus miles an hour going too far? Give us a break."

One of the forensic team, a slight man wearing glasses, addressed Castro. "Sarge, I just checked the acoustics in this room. In addition to those heavy drapes, I'm guessing the walls are soundproofed like the door. Did you notice it when you came in?"

Castro shook his head. "You're saying with the door closed, Hawkins could have shouted at the top of his lungs and nobody could have heard him? " The man nodded. "The housekeeper said it was shut when she came in."

Kenderson had another question: "Sergeant, wouldn't the killer have blood stains on his clothing? Or hands? I didn't see blood on Freddie's clothes."

Castro looked impatient. "Maybe, but the absence of blood doesn't mean the kid isn't the perp. We've got his prints and motive. We just need to check his whereabouts and he's in the bag."

Kenderson frowned. "About the prints; I've been in here with Freddie, and if Earl wasn't around, he liked to pick up the statuette."

Fallon laughed. "More excuses for the poor, little, rich kid?"

Kenderson's face flushed, and he fought hard to keep from telling Fallon to stuff it. Staying on good terms with the police was a must, because if cops got down on the Diversion Center, they could hound his kids into lawless acts. Outside, he tried to run through the camera crews and anchors who thrust mikes under his nose. He ignored them and got in his car, knowing his flight might be on the evening news.

Once behind the wheel, he drove for three blocks and parked in front of one of the upscale homes on Hilltop Terrace

Opening his black report book, he flipped to the information under Hawkins, Freddie. Under phone numbers, he dialed Earl Hawkins' river front realty office in south-west Santa Inglesia. The answering voice sounded impatient and strained. It took a moment to realize he was talking to Arnie Setich, Earl Hawkins' assistant. What was Arnie doing in the riverside office Sunday night, anyway? "Did the police phone you?" Kenderson began, "About your boss?"

The silence unnerved him and he started to repeat the question. "We know." The menacing growl sent a shiver up his back. Kenderson forced himself to continue. "They've arrested Freddie. He's in jail with no alibi. I'm his caseworker. Can you tell me where he was around four this afternoon?"

"Butt out, man, the organization'll take care of Freddie."

Kenderson said, "This is my business, he's a ward in my caseload." He realized a moment later the line had gone dead.

Kenderson sat motionless, looking at the phone. Setich's response jarred him. The man referred to the organization. What organization? Had Hawkins called his realty business an organization? Or was Setich talking about the men he bossed? He suddenly felt the need to talk to someone who would be objective. Fran was too biased about the boy, and his boss, Nate Farber, worried about looking bad, hating any kind of negative publicity. He dialed and punched the Send Button and listened to the five rings. He was about to hit Power Off when the deep voice of Nehi Washington, his friend and colleague from the Diversion Center, answered. "It's me, Jay, I need help. Have you heard the news about Earl Hawkins?" He heard a grunted yes. "They've arrested Freddie and he's probably in an isolation cell at City Jail. He won't cooperate and I tried to get some information from Arnie Setich but he flat told me the organization, whatever that is, would take care of Freddie."

Robert White

After a moment, Washington replied: "Nothing's going to happen tonight. We'll be over tomorrow afternoon for the barbecue and I'll fill you in on Arnie and Pete. They're at the heart of the so-called organization. Also some good advice ... let the cops handle this, okay?"

Kenderson realized Nehi was right but he needed to do something, anything, to find out where Freddie had been during the time of the attack on Earl Hawkins. One comfort, he knew where Freddie was for the night. He drove to the south area of Santa Inglesia, made up of wrecking yards and rundown trailer courts, trying to locate Ermon's home which he knew was in the area. He couldn't remember Ermon's mother's last name and was about to give up when he came up to a sagging trailer with "Murphy" scrawled on the rusting mailbox. Kenderson left the car, walked up the non-existent path, and knocked several times before the door opened. He identified himself but the mother and boyfriend, who both appeared drunk, swore they hadn't seen Ermon all day. Back in the car, he phoned police headquarters but the duty officer said no such person had been picked up.

When he walked in the door, Fran and the kids were full of questions, which he answered briefly. He excused himself after dinner and, sitting in his office, began to list others who might have wanted Earl Hawkins dead. He asked Fran to join him when she could.

The first name was Arnie Setich. Why would he want his boss dead? To take over the business? To avenge an old grudge nobody knew about?

Pete Hawkins: Freddie's adoptive older brother might have ambitions to run the Hawkins empire. He must have resented his father because his brother, Phil, was clearly the old man's favorite.

Sarah MacCormick: Her endless stories, which she insisted on talking about in the weekly parents session, accused Hawkins of cheating her father, Hothar, out of the family fortune, and making his death look like a suicide. She said the man either killed her younger sister, Clarissa, with an overdose of sleeping pills, or drove her to take her own life. At times, he had to cut her off or no one else would have had a chance to talk. Besides, she wouldn't have had the strength to wield the heavy trophy...Or would she? She worked at the mansion and her presence would be taken for granted. She might have gotten behind Earl without him even noticing.

He almost forgot to write down Phil Hawkins' name. What would be his motive? In the course of getting to know Freddie's family and background, he discovered Phil worshiped his father. Kenderson had been warned by others never to criticize Earl in front of Phil. Likewise, Earl was boastfully proud of his eldest. Ironically, the murder weapon was the bronze football trophy Phil had won as an all-state high school quarterback. Kenderson remembered Al Fallon, the wise ass cop, had been a running back on Phil's legendary team, which had won Santa Inglesia's only San Joaquin Regional Championship.

Reluctantly, he added Freddie's name to his list. Was it possible the boy's hate and rage had finally burst through his final barrier of control? Not if Earl had been awake. Could he have been sleeping in his chair? Anything was possible, but Earl Hawkins hadn't risen to prominence by being careless.

Kenderson found himself idly doodling. Was there some mystery person from Hawkins' past that had settled an old score this afternoon? He felt restless and stood up, stretching. Fran came in and asked him what he wanted. "I don't think Freddie killed his adoptive father. I'm listing possible suspects but I'm not getting anywhere. Maybe it's because we're new in Santa

Inglesia and don't have any reliable information about Hawkins' people or his past."

"Honey, I'm afraid the killer is in city jail. I know you're loyal to your kids and hate to see them fail, but Freddie is different."

He started a rebuttal but decided he wasn't going to convince Fran or anyone else. His stomach suddenly tightened with the shocking awareness Freddie wouldn't survive in a twenty-four-hour lockup outside of Oso County. Even in juvenile hall, he'd been treated with kid gloves. What a hell of a mess, he thought. I need to prove his innocence. He felt a sudden chill. The only answer: to find the real killer.

After Fran fell asleep, he lay in bed, mind churning. As a sleuth, he recognized he didn't know what he was doing or was supposed to do. TV detectives had routines. They asked suspects about alibis and in the end, deciphered complicated clues and came up with the killer. Looked easy on the tube. Before dropping off to sleep, he admitted to himself he had nothing to go on but a gut level hunch Freddie hadn't killed Earl Hawkins.

MONDAY MORNING (LABOR DAY)

Fran handed the phone to her sleepy husband, who was working on a bowl of cereal at the breakfast counter. "I thought the voice sounded familiar. Jerry Goldstein, working on a holiday? Something big must be on tap to have Nick Fabretti order his Chief Deputy to get off his duff on a holiday."

Kenderson listened as Goldstein explained his interest. "The DA and I want your opinion about Freddie Hawkins. I hear you told the police Freddic didn't off his old man. Mr. Fabretti is interested why you think the kid is innocent."

After a moment's silence, Kenderson said, "Sure, come on over."

He replaced the phone and turned to Fran. "The DA's office wants my opinion? Why?"

Fran wrinkled her nose. "Because this is an election year, my dear, naive husband. They're hoping you can get their political buns off the hot seat. Like coming up with some reason to keep the Hawkins name out of the media."

A half hour later, Kenderson heard Fran's friendly greeting at the front door, and then an overweight Goldstein entered the kitchen, extending his hand and expressing apologies for intruding. He accepted a cup of coffee from Fran and sat next to Kenderson at the counter.

"Think I must have met you at one or two department retirements." Kenderson gave a brief nod.

"I'll be frank with you, James. Is that what people call you?"

Fran answered. "Jay, mostly."

You told the police you think Freddie Hawkins is innocent." He carefully sipped the hot coffee. "What makes you think that?"

"It's a hunch, a feeling. And something else."

"Like what?" The plump Chief Assistant leaned forward, suddenly alert.

"If Freddie and his adoptive father had been quarreling, and Freddie reached for the trophy in a threatening manner, Earl Hawkins could have easily taken it away from him. He was a powerful man."

Goldstein was silent for a moment. "What if the kid was just fooling around with it and slipped behind Hawkins?"

"No way the man would have let Freddie get behind him with a lethal weapon."

Goldstein frowned in thought. "If Freddie didn't do it, who do you think did?"

"I wouldn't rule out anyone in the family."

Goldstein looked surprised. "You're including the apple of his eye, Phil?" Kenderson nodded.

"Then Pete and Arnie are also suspects?"

"Why not?

"Who else?"

"As far as motive is concerned, I would include Hawkins' sister-in-law, Sarah MacCormick. She's been telling everyone her brother-in-law murdered her father and drove her sister to suicide. She has a strong motive but this is really reaching. She's way too feeble to have wielded a weapon that heavy."

Goldstein shrugged, "Sorry, but the police have no doubts that Freddie bashed in his old man's brains in a fit of rage."

The assistant DA soon left, pausing briefly at the door. "I'll run this by the boss. Sorry to intrude." Kenderson spent the rest of the morning preparing for their guests, but his thoughts gnawed at the puzzle...Who really killed Earl Hawkins?

MONDAY AFTERNOON

Nehi Washington, Kenderson's friend and co-worker, a black psychologist intern who worked as a patrol cop on the night shift, and his wife were expected for an afternoon barbecue. Nehi's wife, Mary, and Fran had become friends soon after the Kenderson's had moved to Santa Inglesia. Their daughters, Cindy and Lillian, turned out to be the top seeds on the Santa Inglesia girl's high school tennis team.

At two o'clock, Nehi, a former defensive end for the University of Pacific, walked into the back yard behind his wife and daughter. Cindy and Lillian squealed greetings and immediately left, chatting about the tennis team. Both ignored Vernon, who conveniently came home too late to help his Dad clean the Weber Pot. The girls went to Cindy's bedroom. Seeing Fran and Mary comparing notes on their kids while preparing steaks and potato salad, Kenderson picked up two beers from the refrigerator and steered Nehi into the office.

The walls displayed his state licenses: Marriage, Family and Child Counselor, and Licensed Clinical Social Worker. Shortly after coming to Santa Inglesia, he had started a part-time counseling practice with demoralized parents. Like those he saw Thursday nights, his private practice couples and single mothers had no idea how to cope with their teenagers. Most had simply given up trying to maintain some semblance of control.

Robert White

Nehi was almost too big for the low naugahide side chair facing the small, three-drawered desk. James rocked back in the yellow upholstered, swivel chair and took a swig of cold beer before speaking. "I need to bounce some ideas off you, okay?" Nehi's spreading grin made his round face beam. "Only as long as the beer holds out. If we're clear on that point, you may proceed."

"I don't think Freddie killed his adoptive father and I need to know about Earl Hawkins' past and present associates. In other words, who else would have wanted him dead?"

Nehi slowly shook his head. "I assumed you wanted to talk about Freddie, about whom you are hugely ambivalent."

Kenderson grimaced. "I know you think I'm overprotective and should make him cooperate. But he doesn't trust any adults, and until I win his confidence, insisting on anything is futile. He just won't respond."

Nehi shrugged. "Someday, maybe you'll try it my way. But back to Freddie."

"He won't deny killing Hawkins, but he doesn't admit it, either. He's just playing head games with the cops. He's forgetting the one person who protected him all his life is dead."

"How much do you know about Freddie's early years?"

"Only what I've learned from the police and probation reports, and Sarah MacCormick's never-ending recitals about Earl's crimes against her family." Nehi nodded.

"Freddie was an expensive present to placate Hawkins' beautiful, twenty-years-younger, childless wife, and to keep her from looking more closely at his hocus-pocus with her family's fortune. Hawkins had no interest at his age in raising an infant son, so he left the job to Clarissa, who was a world class over indulger. The boy had wild tantrums if refused anything. Later, Hawkins was left to bail him out of scrapes with the law and look like a saintly father in the process. About three years, ago a doctor diagnosed Freddie as having Attention Deficit Hyperactive Disorder but I'm sure that's in his case file. I've heard he's been uncooperative with every psychologist and psychiatrist he's been dragged to. Those good souls diagnosed him as everything from a conduct disorder, to an antisocial personality. When he calmed down after taking Ritalin, the ADHD label stuck. What's inside Freddie remains a mystery. He's bright, manipulative and probably looking for someone he can trust. Someone, my friend, who won't let himself be jerked around."

Kenderson nodded and Nehi paused for a moment. "I guess it isn't strange it took so long to diagnose him. His hyperactive behavior and school failures were blamed on his mother and virtually absent father."

Kenderson agreed. "That information helps, but I'm still stuck with the puzzle. "Who would want to kill Earl Hawkins? The man has been hailed as the fount of kindness and charity in this county."

The big man nodded. "I have some ideas, if you're interested. Mary and I are acquainted with some longtime residents of the Meadows. Once they began to trust us, we heard a different kind of story about Santa Inglesia's benefactor. They told us many of the African-American and Mexican-American leaders believe Hawkins, using Arnie Setich as enforcer, has been behind the extortion and protection rackets in the Meadows, our very own ghetto by the Oso river. Small business owners are terrified of his enforcer, so they've never made waves."

Kenderson showed his surprise. "Hawkins, Saint Earl? You're putting me on." Nehi took several swallows of beer.

"Over the years, it was Pete's job to keep the lid on any trouble which, rumor has it, included dropping a few weighted bodies down dry wells. In one case, causing an entire family to disappear. When Ralph Condon, an investigative reporter, his wife and five-year-old daughter vanished, rumors were started he'd moved to escape angry creditors. The owner of the *Sentinal* where Condon worked, said very little except he was puzzled by the sudden flight. Neighbors and friends who swore the family owed no money, suddenly stopped talking. There were hints Condon was working on a piece about Hawkins' background."

Kenderson leaned forward. "Background? What background? Where did he come from?"

"Some old timers say he came here from Chicago. But nobody really knows where to start looking."

"Would someone on the *Sentinel* know Condon's last assignment?" Nehi shook his head. "Maybe, but I heard he sometimes investigated stuff on his own. No one at the *Sentinal* seemed to know exactly what he was doing when he disappeared, or, if they did, were afraid to talk."

Kenderson suddenly stood up. "This is nuts! You're telling me Sarah MacCormick is telling the truth?"

"Essentially. The MacCormick women were beautiful, rich and smart but Sarah sounds so weird, people have quit listening. Most folks figure Hawkins would have gotten rid of her if she were telling the truth."

"How is Hawkins' death going to affect Phil's run for the Senate?

"It's too early to tell. He's contributed a lot of time and money on his own to local charities. He could get hurt at the polls if Freddie is convicted. Most voters won't know or care Freddie isn't a blood relative."

Kenderson leaned forward. "Nehi, you've worked on murder cases, how would you go about finding the killer?"

"First, let me tell you Raul Castro and his homicide squad are among the best in the state. He would have been dumped a long time ago, but the brass who Hawkins owned, know the bought cops under them couldn't find their asses with both hands."

"But Castro and his buddy, Al Fallon, won't consider any other suspect."

"That's what he says, but neither of those guys is a dummy. My advice is to let them handle the investigation."

Kenderson stubbornly shook his head. "I can't just sit back and do nothing. Castro and Fallon might solve the murder someday, but it won't do Freddie any good because he'll be dead. First degree murder will get him a long sentence, starting in the State Youth Authority and then prison. He's too small physically and too brash to survive wherever they put him.

The big man sighed. "You want to play detective?"

"Who else believes he's innocent?"

"Ask. And don't expect anyone to tell the truth. You're going to have to dig and dig and then start all over. It's tough, thankless work. Being a probation officer may open some doors." Nehi wasn't smiling when he stood up. "It could be dangerous. Especially if Pete and Arnie don't want you poking around. And, don't let our esteemed boss know what you're doing."

Nehi reached for his beer. "Do you want my advice?" Kenderson nodded. "Don't try to solve this by yourself. You're a social worker, man, not a cop. Let Castro's guys solve this."

"Would Phil Hawkins support me? Shouldn't I talk to him as soon as possible?"

"He's the one to talk to."

Shouts of "time to barbecue," made them rise and proceed to their backyard cooking assignments. The barbecue proceeded, with Kenderson and Washington broiling steaks for the hungry crowd. Kenderson played the genial host, but in his mind kept visualizing Freddie sitting alone in a barren jail cell.

Robert White

After the Washingtons left, Kenderson returned to the office and put in a call to his ward. The boy wasn't his usual flip self but he turned down Kenderson's offer to visit that night. He reviewed his list of suspects. Who might want Hawkins dead? After two hours, he gave up and spent another restless night in bed. Fran snored gently, but his troubling thoughts kept him awake until an early hour.

TUESDAY MORNING

Kenderson was surprised when Phil Hawkins readily agreed to talk to him in his downtown office before work. On the phone he sounded concerned, saying he hoped with all his heart Freddie wasn't the killer.

Phil was a smaller version of his father, well muscled with an athletic stride, as he advanced to shake hands. He motioned to a chair and returned to his desk. "The police told me you think Freddie's innocent. I'm glad you do, because so do I. In a crazy way, the boy admired my Dad. I agree with what you told the cops. Dad would never have allowed Freddie to get behind him holding that trophy. If he'd acted menacing in any way, Dad would simply have taken it away from him, no problem." Kenderson nodded.

The phone rang, and from the conversation, Kenderson realized the man was busy making funeral arrangements for his father. After Phil hung up the phone, Kenderson stood up, offering to come back later, but Phil waved him back to his seat. Kenderson continued. "Aren't there other people with a motive? Maybe someone from his past?"

Phil looked startled. "From his past? Who said anything like that?" Kenderson shrugged his shoulders. "Doesn't everyone have a past?"

Phil grinned, "Yes, of course. Only Dad's been away from Chicago for over twenty-five years. I was only twelve when we moved to Santa Inglesia."

"Could he have had enemies from his days there?"

Phil paused in thought before resuming. "He talked once about working for an alderman with an odd sounding name, Fetch Crowder, I think it was. But to be honest, I don't believe that's much of a lead. I think Dad's past is a dead end." Looking pensive, he continued with a shake of his head.

"But back to Freddie, I'd like to clear this up for his sake, but, selfishly, mine too. I think the local Democratic slate will suffer in November unless Dad's murder is resolved. What's worse, we could suffer statewide losses if the Republicans want to turn this into a media circus."

Kenderson felt his face grow hot as he forced himself to ask the next question. "I'm sorry to ask, but where were you Sunday night from four to six o'clock?" Hawkins looked startled and then grinned. "Me, you're asking me where I was when Dad was killed? You mean I'm a suspect?" Kenderson felt even more foolish. "Sorry, but my friend who's a cop said I had to ask everybody this question." Hawkins seemed amused. "Well, great, I'm glad you're going to try to clear up this mess." He frowned in thought.

"Well, indeed, where was I?" He seemed to drift off, saying almost to himself, "Yes, I was in Sacramento in the morning at an emergency meeting, then I started back about one o'clock. I wanted a swim and to hit the Jacuzzi, so I stopped at the Elks Lodge about four. I left there a little after five thirty. I had a meeting at six thirty with some campaign people at Bill Foster's ranch outside of town. You want his phone number?"

Relieved, Kenderson said, "I swim at the Elks Lodge at six in the morning when I can. Wakes me up before I go to work. Well, thanks for talking to me. I'll keep you posted." He started to rise, but Phil waved him down again. "Have you talked to Arnie Setich?"

"I phoned yesterday. He told me to butt out."

Phil threw up his hands "I never knew why Dad kept Arnie around. He has the personality of a hyena. Let me ask around. I'll let you know if I find anything helpful, okay?"

They shook hands as Kenderson took his leave, but not before he noticed that Phil seemed to be handling his father's death calmly. Maybe he was still numb from the tragedy and in shock.

Driving back to the converted two story Victorian home, which the Diversion Center shared with the Family Service Agency, Kenderson felt his stomach knot up as he thought about Arnie Setich. The few times he'd met the wiry, graying blond, the man had never smiled and his eyes spoke of barely controlled violence. Afterward, Kenderson had been self-critical, telling himself he had no proof the man was violent and that impressions weren't facts....but the gut feeling remained, Arnie Setich could kill without hesitation or remorse. If Earl Hawkins had earned Arnie's hatred, Kenderson thought, the big man had been doomed. The day and hour he died would depend on Arnie finding a convenient time and an unbreakable alibi to cover himself.

Sitting at his desk littered with case files, Kenderson suddenly felt discouraged. He thought of all the reasons to forget his promise to Freddie. His family didn't deserve the risk of his sticking his nose in where it didn't belong. Nate, his boss, would have his job if he brought blame on the Diversion Center. He had no training as an investigator. He fought down the cramping fear, reminding himself there was no way he could abandon his ward. Freddie, a lifelong pain in everyone's ass, had no friends and his only benefactor was dead.

Sarah MacCormick tried to attend Kenderson's Thursday night group meetings for the parents of his kids. With Freddie's mother dead and her brother-in-law convinced that only a miracle would change his adoptive son, she felt a duty to show up as often as possible. Lately, she'd found it a burden keeping up appearances. She and her sister, Clarissa, had been the toast of the young debs in Santa Inglesia in the days before Earl Hawkins had ruined her family. Feeling out of place at the meetings, she found herself humbly asking the others if they minded her being there because Freddie wasn't really her child and didn't even live with her. Answers were always affirmative. Sometimes anger made her shout that Freddie's troubles were the fault of Earl Hawkins. But mostly she kept quiet, sensing the others were uncomfortable with her tirades. Attending the group meetings was a way of keeping in touch with her sister's precious boy.

When Sarah MacCormick heard the news on the little radio she kept by her bedside, she hoped Freddie was innocent, not that the boy wouldn't have been justified in killing the man. She made a note on the little pad beside her bed to talk to Freddie's caseworker, James Kenderson. She had immediately liked the tall man with the gorgeous hair because he was polite to her and patient with Freddie. She suddenly realized she might be a suspect, after all the things she'd said about Earl Hawkins.

The memory of her first, face to face confrontation with the man, flooded her mind. She'd been overwhelmed with rage when she'd overheard his telephone conversation with Frances Kiplinger, president of the Women's Forum. "I'm helping her because of her insane behavior after Clarissa's death. They were very close," he'd said. His sanctimonious tone enraged Sarah. You drove her to her death, she thought bitterly. You poisoned my father and stole our family's money. Who wouldn't go crazy when nobody would listen to the truth? Right after Clarissa's death, she'd found the courage to go to the County Sheriff, Fred Johnson, a longtime friend of her dead father, to tell him her suspicions. Johnson had listened politely but promised nothing. She found out the next day he'd phoned Earl Hawkins, repeating her conversation. Hawkins had asked her to come into the library. He shut the door.

"When you began accusing me of hurting your family, I blamed it on your grief. Now it's different. Your charges might hurt me a little, but the real damage would be to Phil. I thought you liked him? He can be a State Senator with a bright future ahead of him. Political opponents will use your charges to sully his good name."

She remembered taking a deep breath, glancing at his angry face, and then ducking her head. In a low voice, she'd told him, "You poisoned my father the way you did that Will Blakemore in Chicago. Harold Fisher, a private investigator my father hired to investigate you, found this out. I read a poison register and talked with a doctor. They're pretty sure you used some derivative of Amyl Nitrate that makes the victim appear to be suffering a coronary. They said it would be hard to trace, even with present day technology. You were lucky no one thought to ask for a blood chemistry analysis in either case. You are clever, Earl, but I've found you out. I expect you'll try to kill me. If you do, the Attorney General in Sacramento will receive a sealed envelope documenting your criminal past and the reasons you had me killed."

Earl Hawkins had just grinned at her, and a chill ran down her spine.

"Sarah, face it, people in Santa Inglesia think you're insane. Employers are afraid to hire you. Just stop and think a minute. You need your job here. I've been patient but that's over now. My organization's activities after the elections will be expanding outside the county. People in other sections of the state might take what you say seriously, because they don't know you. I can't and won't let that happen."

His normally quiet voice had grown louder. His meaning was clear, silence or death.

Afterward, she'd stopped talking except in Mr. Kenderson's Thursday night parent meetings. Everything said there, she was assured, would be confidential. He would have known immediately if she'd ignored his warning.

Kenderson turned the pages on Freddie's thick case file, hoping to find a lead he might pursue, when the phone rang.

"Got a minute to talk, Jay?" Nate Farber's tone told him it didn't matter whether he did or not.

"I'm driving to Sacramento for an afternoon meeting, so I'm going to discuss this now. When the DA phones me on a holiday, I know he's very pissed that you didn't cooperate with the police. It makes it look like we coddle criminals at the Center. Remember, the grant committee will meet next week. If they get the idea we're failing to cooperate with law enforcement, next year's money for the Center will be history."

"What about protecting our clients?" Kenderson felt irritated. "I'm willing to cooperate with the police and the DA's office, but that doesn't mean forgetting my responsibilities as a caseworker."

He felt like telling Farber to fuck himself. Instead, he said, "I don't think Freddie Hawkins killed his adoptive father. I'm going to find the real killer."

He waited until Nate finished his sarcastic remarks about the Center not being a detective agency, then added, "Don't worry, I won't do this on County time."

He worked the rest of the morning updating his files and after a quick sandwich, left for the jurisdiction hearing scheduled for one thirty in Judge Simpson's court.

TUESDAY AFTERNOON

Kenderson sat next to Phil Hawkins in a front row of the high-ceilinged courtroom. It was open and shut that Freddie would be tried as an adult, based on the crime and his background as a juvenile, but the official process was mandatory. Kenderson thought about asking the family attorney, Nelson Ivers, to urge the boy's being tried as a juvenile based on his medical diagnosis, but with his father's influence gone, it was an unlikely prospect. Judges throughout the state listened to prosecutors. Most considered defense arguments to be bleeding heart's stuff, and with the public fed up with what they considered wrist slaps for severe juvenile crime, fourteen to sixteen year violent criminals had worn out their options. Kenderson had seen the changing trend, from his earlier experience as a Youth Authority witness, at such jurisdiction hearings.

He'd had a chance to talk briefly with Freddie. The boy was refusing to answer Nelson Ivers' questions. Freddie had been his usual wise-ass self and merely listened to Kenderson's advice without comment. He seemed to be enjoying his growing control over the adults around him. Sitting in the defense section, dressed in baggy orange coveralls with Oso County Detention Center stenciled in black, Kenderson realized how small and harmless Freddie appeared as he squirmed next to his elegantly dressed attorney.

The bailiff called for order and Judge Smithers, a greying man with twenty years on the superior court, climbed the steps to his bench and sat down. A clerk read the petition and Judge Smithers immediately raised the question of jurisdiction. Jerry Goldstein, the prosecutor, declared the boy's present murder charge and previous background precluded his being tried as a juvenile. "Your honor, Freddie Hawkins has proved over the years, and now with this vicious crime, that he is not able to benefit from juvenile services at either the county or state level." Ivers rose and said, "I agree with the prosecution, we are not contesting the issue of jurisdiction at this time. Nor are we seeking bail." The bailiff had risen to his feet at Freddie's rising voice. He and a deputy quickly moved behind the defense table. The bailiff whispered, "Settle down, son, don't make things worse for yourself." But it was too late for reasoning. Ivers felt hands grabbing at his throat. He tried in vain to pry them loose.

"You mother-fucker, you get me out of here." The boy's voice raged. Judge Smithers registered shock. "Bailiff, remove the defendant from court at once. This behavior will not be tolerated!"

Ivers could see Smithers' mouth still forming words but the boy's screams drowned them out. Sharp fingernails bit into his neck as the clawing hands were pried loose. He could hear the bailiff breathing heavily as he attempted to hold Freddie and apply handcuffs. The best he could do was pinion Freddie's left wrist with one cuff. Tugging with the other and aided by another Deputy, the boy was hauled out of court, feet kicking and dragging, shouting "faggots."

Kenderson rose, trailing the trio from the courtroom. He watched the two deputies drag his resisting ward up the Correctional Center bus steps and place him in a seat behind the thick wire mesh which screened the driver from his inmate passengers. He thought of boarding and talking with Freddie, but from experience, he knew the boy would need at least another hour to cool off. He walked to the window where Freddie was sitting. To his surprise, the boy did a thumbs up gesture and grinned at Kenderson. The driver boarded and as the green bus pulled out of the parking lot, Kenderson was in mild shock. Was Freddie playing a game with him, too? He needed to figure out, and fast, how much of Freddie's erratic behavior was real or staged?

Four reporters watching the melee, jotted quickly in note books. He knew his ward's reputation as a world-class mess-up would be raised at least one level.

By the time Kenderson returned to the courtroom it had adjourned and Judge Smithers was heading for the door to his chambers, followed by the two attorneys. As Kenderson neared Ivers, a *Sentinel* reporter, Underwood, approached.

"Counselor," the reporter began,"Why aren't you asking for bail?"

"Not now, Pete, we're due in chambers, I'll talk to you later." Noticing Kenderson, Ivers said, "Wait, I'll want to talk to you about Freddie's case."

The jurist stood behind the walnut desk, too agitated to sit.

"Mr. Ivers, I want an explanation for your client's shocking language and behavior. The young man's conduct is a throwback to the contempt for law and order we witnessed in the sixties radical trials."

"Your Honor, I apologize for his outburst. He's lost the one human being, beside his mother, who stood behind him through all his escapades. I should have advised him before court that his release on bail or recognizance would not be in his or his family's best interests."

"While Earl Hawkins' son has not been before my court, his police record is familiar. In light of that record, I can appreciate your decision. And please know I have the deepest regret for the loss of a good friend, whom I deeply respected. Because of that respect, I would have been willing to release the boy with reasonable assurance he would appear for the preliminary hearing."

Ivers could see the judge was starting to relax, because he sat down in his executive chair and motioned the two attorneys to the upholstered leather chairs in front of his desk.

Nelson Ivers decided to level. "It was partly a political decision to not ask for bail, your honor. Freddie, as you noted, has long been an embarrassment to his family and uncaring as it might seem, keeping him off the streets and out of the limelight, with the elections only two months away, seemed in the best interest of everyone."

Judge Smithers merely nodded.

Ivers pressed his point. "Unwelcome attention will be focused on this case by our political foes. We'll either be accused of favoritism if he's released or of trying to cover up if we keep him locked up." Judge Smithers looked sour.

"I can't tell you gentlemen how deeply I deplore the media's attempt to influence judicial proceedings."

Ivers saw his advantage. "Exactly my feelings, sir, and for that reason, I refrained from explaining my position in open court for fear of biasing the case further with the media. I am thankful you refuse to allow television cameras in your court." Ivers knew TV was Judge Smithers' pet peeve. Ivers thought he should make a further assurance.

"Again, sir, I am sorry for the outburst. I will make sure that my client conducts himself properly in the future."

He could see the doubtful look on the jurist's face. "Gentlemen, let's get to the bottom line on this matter. I have no choice but to arraign the boy. More to the point, what are you going to present at the preliminary hearing? Mr. Ivers?"

"Your honor, we are convinced my client has been charged in error, despite the district attorney's decision to prosecute. He's being tried on his past more than anything else."

"Mr. Goldstein?"

"James Kenderson, Freddie's social worker at the Oso County Diversion Center, is convinced the police are wrong. However, no one else has any doubts about the boy's guilt and a preliminary investigation has turned up no other leads."

Ivers could see the concern grow on Judge Smithers' face. "As both of you know, the preliminary is, for the most part, a legal formality to ensure gross errors have not been made in the arrest process. I must tell you now, Mr. Ivers, unless you can give me reasonable cause for doubting your client is guilty, I will have no choice but to bind the boy over for trial as a adult."

"I am aware you have little latitude to dismiss at the preliminary."

Judge Smithers nodded his head toward Jerry Goldstein. "And you, Mr. Chief Assistant District Attorney, what do you have up your sleeve?"

Ivers saw Jerry grimace. "Sir, Freddie Hawkins had motive, means and opportunity to kill his adoptive father. We have no other suspects simply because other members of his family and staff owed their economic and political success to the man. Eliminating Hawkins would have been like killing the goose that laid the golden egg. Freddie killed on impulse. The others, in my opinion, clearly lacked motive."

The judge raised his eyebrows and stood up. "Thank you gentlemen. Would tomorrow afternoon at one o'clock be too soon for you to present your cases? I can appreciate the need on both sides for an early resolution. I am sure the deceased would also approve the decision."

Nelson Ivers suppressed a smile. It was Smithers' only acknowledgment that he owed his judgeship to the dead Democratic boss.

Kenderson's wait for Ivers was a short one, as promised. The attorney stopped in front of the bench where the social worker had been updating his wards' individual progress notes.

"Judge Smithers was very unhappy with Freddie's outburst. My neck is also scratched to hell. The judge supports my recommendation to leave Freddie in custody until at least the preliminary hearing. That okay with you?"

Kenderson nodded. "I guess so. He needs some time to settle down. When is the preliminary?"

"The judge wants this over with as soon as possible so he set the prelim for tomorrow at one o'clock."

Ivers started to walk away and then turned back. "Arnie Sctich phoned me early this morning and made a big deal out of keeping Freddie in custody. I don't understand why he's suddenly interested. He's always dismissed the kid as a flake. Anyway, I followed his instructions because there's no one else with authority to issue orders."

"How about Phil?"

"He's never been part of day to day operations. He has no choice but to leave decisions to Arnie. It could change later."

Kenderson gathered his notebook and followed Ivers out of the courthouse wondering, like Ivers, why Hawkins' assistant was suddenly concerned about keeping Freddie locked up.

Robert White

At three o'clock, Sarah MacCormick, who had devoted time to making herself look attractive, entered her gray Honda Civic, drove west, and minutes later pulled up in one of the Diversion Center's parking spaces. The young lady at the reception desk asked if she had an appointment and when she shook her head, the receptionist spoke through an intercom. A few moments later, she smiled as Kenderson appeared.

Once seated, she suddenly felt nervous. "Mr. Kenderson, I'm sorry I missed last Thursday's meeting but I was just getting over a bad cold."

He smiled and asked what could he do for her.

She heard the indignation rising in her voice: "I am so shocked by the newscasters naming Freddie as Earl Hawkins' killer. I heard you are the only one who thinks he's innocent. Well, I just wanted you to know, I do too."

"Thanks for your support."

Sarah MacCormick suddenly felt uneasy. Was Mr. Kenderson defending Freddie because he had a soft heart? Was she, too, fooling herself about her nephew, blind to what he had become? Her mind returned to the beautiful little boy sitting at Clarissa's knee listening to fairy stories. But time and hatred of his adoptive father had changed him. She felt she could no longer deny the terrible truth. Her nephew, the light of her dead sister's life, might have lost control and killed Earl Hawkins. Her throat ached as bitter tears began to flow.

"Mr. Kenderson, could Freddie have done it? Could it have been because of drugs?"

"Sarah, I don't think Freddie killed his adoptive father. I'm looking into other suspects, including you." She noted his smile and returned her own.

"Oh! Well, everybody in town knows how I felt about Earl Hawkins but I didn't kill him." She dabbed at her eyes with a tissue.

She realized her voice had become shrill. "Not that I didn't think of it after what he did to my father and sister."

"I've heard those rumors before. Many of them, I understand, started by you. If they are true, why haven't the police or district attorney's office taken action?"

Sobs muffled her words. "Because I am a foolish woman who didn't have the sense to keep quiet until she had proof. All I succeeded in doing was convince the authorities and most everyone, even former friends, I'm a mental case." She paused to wipe her eyes.

"I don't blame you or the police for not believing me. Accusing a man most people believe is a saint...." She stopped to wipe her eyes. "Very soon, though, I should have the evidence to prove Earl Hawkins was a swindler and a killer who controlled Oso County politics through blackmail threats." Kenderson leaned forward.

"What proof?"

"Please be patient and hear me out. A private detective, Harold Fisher, was hired years ago by my father, who'd begun to be suspicious of Earl Hawkins. After my father's death, Fisher continued on his own to investigate Hawkins' background, maybe hoping to use the information to blackmail the man. Three years ago, Fisher phoned saying he had information he wanted to sell, demanding fifty thousand dollars. I was happy and angry at the same time. I told him I barely existed on Earl Hawkins' charity job and couldn't pay him fifty dollars, let alone fifty thousand. I must have sounded hysterical, so he hung up."

Kenderson silently wondered if this was the truth. She continued: "I overheard Fisher on the phone the next day--as the receptionist I could listen in if I was careful--offer Earl Hawkins the same amount of money to forget what he had uncovered in his investigation. Shortly afterward, Fisher disappeared from

Santa Inglesia. Rumor said he ran away to escape the wrath of an angry husband. He *was* a ladies man, but I know Earl Hawkins ordered Pete to kill Fisher, but the job was botched according to a shouting match I overheard when the library door was ajar. I believe Harold Fisher is alive. He told me once, if he ever retired he'd move to Arizona, so I've run a personal ad in the *Arizona Republic* in Phoenix, asking him to contact me. Fisher's information may uncover enemies from his past. Wouldn't that help Freddie?"

Kenderson nodded. "It certainly would. But what about Phil and Pete? Could either of them have a motive to kill their father?"

Sarah shook her head. "Earl Hawkins was Phil's hero. If anyone questioned Earl, Phil became almost irrational and would angrily defend his father's actions."

"What about Pete? If he is capable of killing a stranger, couldn't he have attacked his father in a rage?"

"Maybe, because he always resented Earl's favoring Phil. But Pete feared his father. He would have had to be desperate."

"And his pal, Arnie Setich?"

"There's a dangerous man. Maybe he wanted to take over the whole operation. Maybe he was in cahoots with someone from Earl's past. Fisher's information could help us. I hope he'll answer my ad."

Kenderson nodded. He'd heard the police talk about Phil's and Pete's alibis at the time of the murder. Phil was at the Elk's Lodge using the Jacuzzi and Pete and Arnie said they were playing poker at a downtown card club. Could the two be covering for one another? Kenderson knew he couldn't wait for Sarah MacCormick's real or mythical Mr. Fisher to appear. He'd have to find a way to check on Hawkins' past himself. Sarah MacCormick rose from her chair.

"Thank you for not giving up on my nephew. I know he's been a problem to work with." She paused, wondering if she should say more. She opened her purse and fumbled for her wallet. From it, she took a snapshot of Freddie sitting on his mother's lap and handed it to Kenderson. "Those were happy times." Kenderson marveled at the beatific expressions on the face of the attractive mother and the handsome little boy. How harsh the changes since that moment in time. Sarah went on.

"I was on the upstairs landing the day Earl Hawkins nearly slapped the boy to death. From then on, Freddie and his mother changed. She kept Freddie away from Earl because she realized she was powerless to protect him. Our father was dead, our assets controlled by Hawkins, even our family attorneys, who were supposed to help us, backed away. A week before she died--I say killed--my sister told me to watch out for Freddie if anything happened to her." She fought against the welling tears, wanting to finish quickly. "By then Freddie had changed, too. He was eaten up by hatred and we had spoiled him, giving in to most of his demands. It was our mistaken way of compensating for Earl's cruelty. After that one horrible beating, the man hardly even spoke to the boy. As he got older, Earl Hawkins tried once or twice to make amends and involve Freddie in his crooked business. For several weeks, Freddie joined Pete and Arnie when they had their so-called weekly sales meetings, and sometimes he accompanied them on assignments in the Meadows. No wonder the boy hangs out with the prostitutes there. They were probably the only ones who treated him half-way nice. The poor boy doesn't know who to trust and it was the last straw when the doctors found out he's suffering from this attention deficit disorder."

She shook her head. "Freddie knows a lot about the real Hawkins' organization. If Arnie and Pete fear he'll incriminate them in the course of the trial, he'll be killed and it will look like some kind of accident."

Sarah's words came as a shock to Kenderson. Surely the boy would be safe in jail. But Nehi Washington, and now Sarah MacCormick, were painting a frighteningly different picture of Santa Inglesia. How far would Earl Hawkins' survivors go to protect their illicit dealings? And how far reaching was that empire?

His mind spinning from what he'd learned, Kenderson walked to the front door with Sarah. He said goodbye and watched as she got into her car. Returning to his office, he felt a sudden urgency to visit Freddie and to check on his safety. First thing tomorrow, he would make time to visit the special unit at the Oso County Correctional Center where the boy was being held.

Back in his office, Kenderson realized he needed information about Hawkins' past in Chicago, and waiting for Sarah MacCormick's real or imaginary private eye to provide it, seemed too chancy. He recalled Howard Marinovich, a colleague from Chicago who had been in graduate school with him at the University of California, Berkeley. They'd met again at a recent National Association of Social Workers' conference in Los Angeles, where talk about graduate school days over beers had been enjoyable. After exchanging phone numbers, they'd agreed to keep in touch. He got the receptionist at the Child Protective Services office in Chicago and left the message: "Please tell him it's urgent that he phone. Tell him a client of mine is wrongly accused of murder, and I need some information about the victim." He left both his office and home phone numbers.

His thoughts turned to Pete and Arnie. How was he going to check on their whereabouts? First, he had to find out what Sergeant Castro had to say about their alibis. After a fifteen minute delay, he heard the Sergeant's impatient voice.. "Their alibis? Are you kidding? The bums they hang around with at the card parlor will corroborate anything those two say."

"Are they suspects?"

"Sure, but it's not very likely either one of them offed Hawkins. They owed him, like a lot of other people in town. He was their bread and butter."

He was about to ask Castro if he thought Freddie would be safe at the Correctional Center but changed his mind. In Santa Inglesia, people thought of Freddie Hawkins as someone they wanted to be safe from.

Kenderson was concentrating on the psychological and psychiatric reports in Freddie's file when the phone rang and he heard the welcome voice of Howard Marinovich asking him how he could be of help.

"Howard, thanks for returning my call." He summarized the events before and after Earl Hawkins' death. "One of Hawkins' sons mentioned his father had worked for a Chicago Alderman by the name of Fetch Crowder. This was probably twenty-five years ago. Would newspaper morgues have any information about people who had worked for the Alderman? Most newspapers here on the West coast keep microfilms of past editions. I'll give you our fax number at home, and thanks for any help you can give me...and I owe you one."

Marinovich's assurance he would check out the old issues, made Kenderson feel he was finally making progress.

Phoning the Hawkins' mansion, he hoped he could make an appointment to talk to Pete. Pete answered gruffly and told him he had a few minutes if Kenderson could get his ass over fast.

Getting answers from the oldest son of Earl Hawkins was like pulling teeth. To Kenderson's question about who Pete thought might have killed his father, he grunted that it was probably asshole Freddie. "The kid is nuts and goes ballistic over nothing. I figure the old man must have been on the phone or looking away when the kid slugged him. Probably some beef over his car or allowance. If it was me, the kid would have damn well earned what he got, not bribed to keep from fucking up."

Kenderson could see no sign of grief on the man's face. He took a deep breath. "So where were you when your Dad was killed? Between four and six o'clock?" Kenderson braced for Pete's indignant thunder but the latter remained calm. He must be used to such questions from the cops.

"Me and Arnie Setich were playing low-ball down at Flaherty's Card Room. You can ask a dozen guys down there."

"Did you leave at any time?"

"Sure, I ran some errands later in the afternoon but I was only gone for about a half hour."

Before Kenderson could speak, Pete volunteered. "The guys in the cardroom can vouch for that."

From what Nehi had told him, plus Castro's comments, he figured Pete would have an airtight alibi no matter what he'd been doing.

"Where can I find Arnie Setich?" Pete showed surprise. "Why you want to talk to him? I told you we was playing lowball at Flaherty's."

Kenderson forced down a strong urge to get out of Pete's sight but he thought of Freddie sweating out a long prison term. "Hey, Pete, I'd like to talk to him myself, okay?"

Pete shrugged. "So call this number. I don't think he'll want you buttin' in our business." He reached in his shirt pocket and handed Kenderson a business card.

A glance at the card showed both Pete's and Arnie's names as sales reps for Hawkins Reality. Each had a different phone number.

"Thanks for your time," Kenderson said as he left the library. Opening the heavy oaken front door, he walked out feeling relieved.

Kenderson parked at the end of MacCormick street which dead ended at the Oso River, and began looking for 15 Front Street. Front turned out to be a narrow, block-long stretch of cracked cement with a removable barrier, and sealed at the other by a twelve-foot high cyclone fence. Dense Oleander bushes grew on the river side of the street. Number 15 was the sole building on the block and certainly didn't look like a realty office. Setich's refusal to explain how to get to 15 Front Street, when he phoned for an appointment, became clearer. The man figured I'd give up. Until five minutes ago, when he'd spotted the barely readable Front Street sign, Kenderson had decided he'd been given a false address.

Walking to the entrance of the two story edifice, Kenderson couldn't locate a front door on the ground floor facing the street. He started to walk up steep wooden stairs to the second landing when Arnie Setich suddenly appeared at the top. The thin face was expressionless. "I'll talk from here."

In the long silence that followed, Kenderson felt his stress scale going off the chart. At least delinquent kids talked, but this man gave off a feeling of unadulterated hostility. Standing awkwardly, Kenderson dove in. "Frankly, I'm checking alibis. I don't think Freddie killed his father." Stony silence. He plunged on. "Pete says you and he were playing cards at Flaherty's. He said he left for a half hour around four o'clock." Setich's stare unnerved him, as did the silence. "Is that what you recall?" He felt his resolve waver.

After what seemed an age, Setich nodded. His "Check it out" was also a curt dismissal. Kenderson felt foolish to be thanking the guy but doing so was an automatic reflex in his trade. He felt air leaking out of his lungs, suddenly aware he'd been holding his breath for most of the brief interview. As he turned to walk down the steps, he finally understood why no one challenged Setich's deadly stare and intimidating body language.

How could Hawkins have successfully posed as a benevolent saint for years, and let a thug like Setich represent him? His recent encounters with Arnie convinced him that victims, present or past, would be very, very reluctant to talk to the authorities or anyone else. It also occurred to Kenderson that confining his extortions to the Meadows' merchants was how Hawkins was able to fool the rest of the population into believing he was a saint. Arnie simply convinced Meadows' victims that talking was a fatal thing to do.

Walking back to his car parked on MacCormick, he wondered about the strange outside structure of 15 Front Street. No ground floor entrance? Did prospective buyers really have to climb steep steps to do business with Hawkins Realty. It occurred to Kenderson they must not have any elderly buyers. What was inside that Arnie didn't want him to see? Relieved to be away from the weird, isolated structure, and the stone cold Setich, Kenderson drove home pondering what to do next.

TUESDAY EVENING

He kissed Fran, who was preparing dinner. He guessed the kids were in their rooms, Cindy no doubt on the phone with her boy friend. Vernon had just upgraded his 386 IBM Clone to 486 and was into Internet, big time. I love my family, he thought, but should I tell them the mess I'm in? Fran was against "coddling" Freddie. Her job in the DA's office had influenced her toward a "law and order" approach to most social issues. The kids probably thought Freddie was a nerd, or geek, or whatever the current term was for loser.

He wanted to talk about the events of the day, but didn't. Fran's views tended to be simplistic. For her, there were few extenuating circumstances or softening of judgments.

Dinner followed with Cindy and Vernon lamenting the start of school the following Monday. Vernon asked if Freddie had committed the murder and Kenderson said he didn't think so, and was about to expand on his reasons for coming to this conclusion when the phone rang. Cindy and Vernon looked expectant, Fran annoyed, as he stood up. "I'm expecting a call, okay?" he said. The kids seemed disappointed, even though they shared a separate line between them.

The voice was Marinovich's. "Got some stuff that should interest you. Our office is close to the *Chicago Tribune* and I started in mid-sixties on their microfilm. There's a couple of

articles which should interest you. By the way, the name w
be Hawkins but Hankins. If you have a fax, I'll get it to
right away."

Kenderson thanked him and said that the fax and p
numbers were the same.

For the teenagers, not answering the phone, even th ugh
they knew it was for the fax, was an obvious hardship. Hurrying
through dinner, he went back to the office. Two faxed ages
were in the machine and he quickly read the contents.

The first article mentioned an Earl Hankins as as ant
to a Fetch Crowder, Alderman in one of the South side di icts.
There was a disturbance at one of the Alderman's political
campaign meetings that eventually ended in the police being
called. No arrests were made and Hankins was publicly
complimented by his boss for using "restrained force" on the
hecklers to restore order.

The second article described a tragic and unexpected
death at a campaign luncheon before members of a culinary
union, in which Crowder and his opponent, Will Blakemore
were slated to speak. At the end of lunch, Hankins, according
to witnesses, allegedly poured a fresh cup of coffee for his
bosses' rival. A few moments after reaching the podium,
Blakemore collapsed before he could even start his speech. The
hotel doctor failed to revive the politician and pronounced his
death the result of a coronary occlusion. Blakemore's wife and
two sons swore their father was in perfect health. His backers
accused Crowder and his assistant of poisoning their candidate.
The investigation ground to a halt when the coffee cup from
which Blakemore drank could not be located. Hankins was
accused of destroying the evidence. The account ended with
angry comments by the Blakemore sons that the issue was far
from over. An autopsy, the article concluded, failed to reveal
any evidence of a fatal poison and the matter was dropped.

Kenderson re-read both items carefully and then did some calculating. If Hawkins, then Hankins, left Chicago roughly twenty-five years ago, the reason for his exodus was now clear. Had the Blakemore sons found their father's killer and settled the old score last Sunday night? He felt a moment of elation. Now he had one concrete motive. Someone besides Freddie wanted the man dead. A moment later, he felt letdown when it occurred to him that Hankins had done very little to hide his identity. Hankins to Hawkins, and kept his first name the same? Big deal. It wouldn't have taken an agency with nationwide operatives very long to locate Hankins/Hawkins.

He thought of phoning Castro and then changed his mind. He could hear the Sergeant: "Twenty five years they waited to kill the man? Give me a break."

He argued with himself. If Hawkins was behind the extortions in the Meadows, he's made a lot of enemies. One of them could have finally taken revenge.

He quickly dialed the Washington home and from their daughter, Lillian's, disappointed tone, he guessed she was hoping to hear from a younger, more exciting caller. When Washington answered he gave him a quick rundown on the new information. "So how are you going to follow up on this?" Kenderson could hear the doubt in his friend's voice. He realized he had not thought it through. Washington let the silence hang before he went on: "Granted this is true, how do you think Arnie and Pete and Phillip are going to react to your releasing this information? It's old news, Jay. Hawkins' attorneys will point out the man was never charged, let alone convicted of a crime. I know you didn't ask for my advice, but you've got to start with Freddie. If he won't cooperate and tell you where he was, you're nowhere, right, and grabbing at straws."

He must have been restlessly turning in bed because just before turning out the light, Fran said. "Quit fretting, honey, it will all come out in the wash, as my Mom used to say."

He thought sourly, thanks for your support.

WEDNESDAY MORNING

Nate Farber was waiting for him when he entered the front door of the Victorian. He ushered Kenderson into his office and closed the door. "Freddie Hawkins is in the hands of law enforcement for a major felony. So we, the Oso County Diversion Center, and specifically you, are no longer involved in his case so I want you to close it. Need I say more?"

Kenderson nodded, not trusting himself to speak. What Farber was ordering was unethical and an ass-saving ploy. Social workers did not abandon their clients because they were an embarrassment. Juvenile Probation Officers did not abandon their wards until a Superior Court ordered their status changed. Tight lipped, Kenderson nodded again and left before he got into Farber's face and got his ass fired. He knew he must see Freddie immediately and prepare him for the legal confusion ahead. And if Sarah MacCormick was right, to make sure the County Correctional Center was safe.

Kenderson sat close to Freddie in the crowded, noisy D Unit Control Room at the Oso County Correctional Center, holding the portable phone on his lap. A hassle about where to interview his ward was finally approved by the Center's Superintendent. He had to raise his voice to be heard and realized with relief that the two control officers weren't listening.

"These punks know it don't pay to mess with me." Freddie was off on a macho trip, which Kenderson ignored.

His attention was focused on the faces of the D Unit inmates through the glass partition, young men in their twenties and thirties sitting bored in front of a big TV set, bolted to a six-foot high stand in the corner of the day room. This was his ward's only visual contact with the older inmates, other than at mealtime. When the others were locked up, Freddie was allowed in the day room to exercise. When the adult inmates were out of their cells, Freddie remained confined to a segregated isolation room consisting of a metal toilet and basin with hot and cold water, plus a locker for his clothes.

How could anyone harm him in this protected arrangement, Kenderson thought with relief. He also guessed Freddie's reputation as a jail house nut must have preceded him. Freddie was saying, "It's the only way to do time, man. Make the punks afraid of you."

Kenderson guessed Freddie must be taking his Ritalin because he was at least making sense. He let the boy brag about being a bad dude for awhile before he asked, "Freddie, why did you give me a thumbs up and a grin on the bus. Were you putting on a show?"

Freddie grinned again. "It's how you make it in jail. If you act wild and crazy, nobody will mess over you."

"Do you put on acts for me?" Kenderson asked. Freddie was silent for a moment, and then grinned. "Sometimes, man, sometimes."

Kenderson let out his breath. "It's okay to be up front with me, okay?" Kenderson pondered how to ask his next question. He decided there was no best way.

"How much did you learn about your adoptive Dad's organization? Your Aunt Sarah says you used to accompany Pete and Arnie on their trips to the Meadows."

It surprised Kenderson to see Freddie's normal surly look change to sudden fear."Hey, man, don't ask me nothin' about that stuff. I ain't said nothing to nobody. And I ain't about to. Arnie knows I won't snitch and so does Pete."

"Freddie, you've got to be out front with me if I'm going to help you. Do you think Arnie Setich would stop you from testifying if you go to trial?"

Freddie looked panicky. "He knows I won't say nothing."

"But what if he's worried about what you might say under intense cross-examination?"

"Shit! You trying to scare me?"

Kenderson pondered his next question for so long that Freddie asked, "What?"

"Have you seen anyone in here connected with Arnie Setich?"

Kenderson could see the question alarmed him, but he tried to cover it up with his with his usual cool. "I can take care of myself." The boy's strained voice belied his brave words.

"Then you have recognized somebody?"

Kenderson watched Freddie's struggle between his need to be tough, and a sixteen year old who suddenly finds himself way beyond his depth.

"A guy named Simstead just shows up and suddenly he's a trustee. He's the only one allowed to bring my food tray and medicine. I remember him hanging around with Pete and Arnie when I was a kid."

"I thought you had to put in months of good time before you made trustee?"

"That's right! So something stinks!" Freddie raised voice brought curious looks from the two officers.

"Keep it down," Kenderson urged quietly. His head reeled.

Somebody very high up in the sheriff's department had to have arranged for Simstead's overnight booking and elevation to trustee. It was important neither he nor Freddie let on they recognized the man. In a low voice, Kenderson asked Freddie which inmate was Simstead. "Don't point. Just tell me which chair he's sitting in."

"He's on the fourth chair to the right of the TV." Kenderson stole a quick glance at a husky looking guy with a flattop haircut. Was this man, under instructions, waiting to kill Freddie? Jail and prison homicides were easier to cover up because inmate witnesses were universally afraid to talk. His thoughts raced. What were his options? Talk to Sheriff Fred Johnson? If Johnson had connections to Setich, it would put Freddie in even greater jeopardy. Petitioning a judge to order a transfer back to Juvenile Hall, or temporarily to the Youth Authority, was out of the question. Freddie's past actions, real or put on, had labeled him incorrigible and a high risk for escape.

He thought of appealing to the Attorney General's office in Sacramento. Would they intervene if they thought his ward was in real danger? What kind of evidence would they demand? He felt a sudden letdown, realizing whoever he phoned would insist on talking with Nate Farber, who'd inform them Freddie Hawkins had been dropped from the Diversion Center caseload. He thought of Phil Hawkins and suddenly felt a ray of hope.

He checked in his report book and found Phil's office number and dialed on his portable. The ringing continued and Kenderson expected to get a voice mail response but none came and, disappointed, he hung up.

Kenderson thought about phoning Nick Fabretti, the county District Attorney. He shelved that idea because it was common knowledge the latter was supported by Hawkins in the last election. Somehow, he had to get his ward out of the Correctional Center. But how? With a major felony charge pending, he would never be allowed to remove Freddie from the confines of the County Correctional Center.

He became aware Freddie was eyeing him with a puzzled expression. "You go somewhere?"

"No, I'm still here." He thought, could he free the boy during his court appearance this afternoon? The bailiffs in Judge Smithers' court wouldn't be suspicious. They'd seen him often enough from his court appearances with wards in his custody. He hard-eyed Freddie and said. "Listen, and don't flip out and don't make a noise, okay? How would you go about escaping from court this afternoon?"

He could see Freddie wanting to brag about his past escapes, but cold reality won over. He responded slowly."Can you get Ivers to ask the judge if they'll take off the leg irons and cuffs?"

Kenderson nodded. He guessed Judge Smithers wouldn't be concerned about the boy's escaping with two, six foot, armed deputies standing behind him.

"Then what?"

"No need to know. Just start hollering and chasing me when I make a break for it. Be clumsy, man, you've got a limp, use it. Fall down in front of those asshole deputies so maybe you'll trip one or both of them."

Kenderson shook his head in disbelief. I'm a peace officer and I'm planning a felony escape? But what other options did he have? Letting Freddie be murdered was not one of them. I'll phone Phil again, maybe he can intervene with Setich.

He dialed Phil Hawkins' number again and realized he was holding his breath, wanting desperately to talk to Phil, or leave an urgent message on the answering machine. He finally hung up, trying to hide his discouragement.

Now, Freddie's plan had to be it. Kenderson had a final question. "If you make it,where will you hide out?"

"I'll phone you, okay?"

Kenderson suddenly realized abetting an escape was going to be frighteningly real in a few short hours. He decided he had better be prepared. "Freddie those deputies are younger and faster than I am. Can you signal me when you're ready to go, so I can be ready?"

The boy grinned, obviously enjoying the prospect of his social worker helping him split from court. "How about I cough, twice?"

Kenderson nodded, silently praying a legal way to save his ward could be found. Where was Phil? And why no voice mail?

He quickly reviewed the plan with Freddie before walking to the parking lot, feeling like a stranger he didn't even know. He wanted to talk to Nehi, but knew it would be wrong to involve his cop friend in a criminal act.

Kenderson's thoughts ran wild as he sat at his desk back at the Diversion Center. What am I doing? I'm a badge-carrying peace officer, about to commit a felony which could end my career and freedom. In despair, he realized the nightmare would never end, nor Freddie be safe, until Earl Hawkins' murderer was uncovered. Reaching into the small upper drawer of his desk, he pulled out a copy of his suspect list. His eye, as usual, focused on Arnie Setich's name. He was the logical suspect. Arnie wouldn't have aroused suspicion if he'd entered the library on the pretext of wanting to find a document. He could have easily gotten behind Hawkins, grabbed the heavy trophy, and bludgeoned the older man to death. He would know that Freddie had handled the trophy numerous times, so he would have worn gloves to avoid leaving fingerprints. The biggest puzzle was the motive. Why would Arnie suddenly kill his boss? Was he paid by Will Blakemore's sons to avenge the murder of their father? Twenty five years after the fact? Not likely. Had there been a falling out recently? Over what? Could Sarah MacCormick have heard anything at the office that would shed light on a motive? He would ask her right away.

Kenderson was about to hang up when Sarah MacCormick answered, and he identified himself. "Sorry," she said, "I was out the door when I heard the phone. I was going to drive out to the Center to visit Freddie." He felt a rush of anxiety. Complications they did not need.

"Freddie will be coming to town this afternoon at one o'clock for his preliminary hearing."

"Oh, should I be there?"

Kenderson wanted to shout, Absolutely not! Instead he said: "It's just a formality. Be over in a few minutes and they'll take Freddie right back to the Center." The escape plan was chancy enough. Sarah MacCormick would insist on sitting directly behind the boy and could get hurt when Freddie fled from the courtroom.

He was relieved when she said she'd visit him later in the day. Kenderson jumped in, "Sarah, could anything you overheard at the office give you any idea why Arnie Setich might want to kill his boss?"

After a strained silence, she said, "Some kind of a new project was on the fire. I didn't hear any details but my impression was that Earl was planning to expand his organization."

Kenderson felt his heart pump faster. "Did Earl threaten to cut Setich out? Anything like that?"

"I've heard nothing, but everyone's been irritable these past few weeks. There were serious disagreements, that's all I know."

But what was the actual plan? He wondered if there were details he could get his hands on. He asked Sarah.

"I never saw anything in writing because I'm sure what was being planned was illegal. I'm still working at the mansion. I'll keep my eyes and ears open and let you know if I learn anything more." Kenderson saw the puzzle starting to take shape as he hung up.

WEDNESDAY NOON

Kenderson didn't feel hungry, but made himself eat the low-fat, turkey cold cut on the fresh rye bread Fran had made on their new Zojiruchi Home Bakery the night before. He felt himself wavering, and knew he had to settle his nerves before court. As he had done in the past, he drew a blank piece of paper from his drawer and drew a line down the middle of the page. On the left side, he listed the reasons why he had to help Freddie escape. He wrote: *The boy will surely be killed, once he returns to the Correctional Center.*

Why are you so sure? He wrote: *No way could a new inmate become an overnight trustee, and assigned to work with the one juvenile on D Unit, unless orders came from a high official.*

An opposite thought occurred. He wrote: *Could Simstead be there to protect Freddie?* Who from? He decided that his last thought was reaching.

He returned to the left side of the page and wrote: *Maybe the deputies and the judge will think I'm just clumsy.*

He decided he had to make his limp more pronounced when he entered the Courtroom.

He dialed Phil Hawkins' office and hung up after fifteen rings. Why no receptionist, why no answering service, why no voice mail? Had somebody threatened Phil, demanding he stay away from the trial and further contacts with him or Freddie?

He phoned Ivers's office and, after identifying himself to both secretaries, he heard the attorney's voice. "I've been trying to reach Phil. Do you know where he is?"

"I heard he was called to Sacramento yesterday. Some political meeting. He didn't leave a number where he could be reached. Why do you want to talk to him?"

He considered the risks of letting Ivers know his concerns, so decided to make his question general. "I'm always worried about Freddie's hurting someone or getting himself hurt."

Ivers' voice was suddenly alert. "Have you heard anything?"

Kenderson decided to let the matter drop. "Nothing, just my usual concerns for the kid."

Ivers sounded relieved, convincing Kenderson he could no longer be sure who to trust. He was about to disconnect when he remembered Freddie's request and cursed himself for almost forgetting. "Counselor, Freddie wanted his leg chains and handcuffs removed during court. Will the judge allow it?"

Ivers laughed. "I'll ask him. I'm sure those two big deputies can handle a hundred fifty pound kid, even if I can't."

The stiff collar on his dress shirt rubbed uncomfortably against the nail scratches, as Nelson Ivers waited, phone in hand, for a Correctional Officer to summon his client Freddie to the phone. He didn't expect an apology, and got none, when the boy answered, "What?"

"You'll be out on the streets by tonight. Just checking to see you're okay and not mad about yesterday. Admit it, Freddie, you aren't the most reliable person on earth, okay? So don't do anything crazy. If you stay mellow through today, I'll see you start getting good bucks from your Dad's estate."

Ivers was pretty sure the promise of money would keep the kid cool until after court. After that, it wouldn't matter.

Freddie didn't buy Ivers' promise. He was going to do his own thing, like always. At noon, in the mess hall, he barely touched the cold cuts and potato salad served on a partitioned metal tray by Simstead. The guy let him know he'd hidden some marijuana under a strip of tape under his tray. "It's good stuff, kid, enjoy."

He didn't bother to look.

Freddie flopped on the bed in his room on D Unit and began thinking about Simstead. He'd noticed the guy right away because he didn't look like the other losers. Somebody, probably the guy who offed the old man, wanted him dead, too. Was that Pete or Arnie? Whatever, if he was dead, the case would be closed. He knew the guy would be watching him every second, ready to create a "fatal accident" or a suicide.

Once out of the courtroom, he knew the place nobody would think of looking for him. He leafed through the Penthouse magazine he'd been reading before noon chow but his mind was racing. He could see himself bolting past the stupid bailiffs. He knew they wouldn't shoot in the courtroom. One thing in his favor, everybody thought he was a lame brain because of his ADHD. He hoped his PO would fall on his ass at the right time.

WEDNESDAY NOON

Brad Miller, a reporter for the prestigious monthly magazine, *California Now*, sat opposite Barbara Diaz, a pretty, dark-haired reporter for the *Santa Inglesia Sentinel*. She looked at the overweight journalist with ill-concealed impatience. He smiled. "My boss wants me to do a background piece on your late Democratic strongman, Earl Hawkins. That's why I'm asking for your time. Can you help me? I'll be glad to share what I turned up on his Chicago background." Barbara Diaz sat up a little straighter.

"His name was Hankins then." Unhurriedly, he continued: "I spent some years on the *Chicago Tribune* so I learned first hand the hocus-pocus of Chicago's Democratic political machine. In that enchanted city there are political districts called wards, run by aldermen. The latter are viewed by constituents as combination Saint Nick's, social workers and parish priests. The alderman, through his well paid ward-heelers, is literally everything to everyone, meaning, of course, the party faithful. That is where and how Earl Hankins, now Hawkins, learned his trade. Opponents of his boss claimed he'd poisoned their candidate, a Mr. Will Blakemore, during a union meeting luncheon where both candidates were scheduled to speak. From what I've learned, it looks like the man transferred his political and extortion skills to this humble

California city on the Oso River. He also did time in Joliet Prison for a series of burglaries he committed, with the connivance of several corrupt cops. He left behind an unlamented, hopelessly alcoholic wife and mother of his two sons."

"Shit," Barbara Dias said. "Hawkins has been on the up and up with the Afros and Latinos in this town. They've supported him and his candidates every election. Why wouldn't they? The other side are flat-out racists."

"So Earl Hawkins has been good to minorities. But what about the accusations he's behind the protection rackets in the Meadows."

He watched doubt grow on her face.

"How could the man fool everyone? I don't buy that crap. He would have been brought down through public pressure a long time ago. My paper would never stand for that....if they could prove it." She finished the sentence on a lowered note.

As he stood to leave, he told her: "Didn't you have a colleague who's family disappeared? Guy by the name of Condon, who was working on a Hawkins background piece before he and his family suddenly vanished. And what's very strange, neither he nor any family member has ever sent a postcard to long-time friends or colleagues. I know, I checked."

The dark-haired woman sighed. "That's always bothered me. The guy was quiet and did his own stuff, but he helped me a lot when I was getting started."

The woman watched him leave, feeling strangely tense and unhappy.

WEDNESDAY AFTERNOON

Kenderson looked at his watch and was surprised to see he hadn't much time before Freddie's one o'clock preliminary hearing. He started to leave when Nate Farber walked through the front door, scowling. "Where are you going?"

"Freddie's preliminary hearing is at one o'clock." The scowl deepened. "We've dropped the kid from our rolls. You're off the case, period."

He felt a sudden surge of relief. He wanted to laugh aloud. He wouldn't have to become a criminal because his boss wouldn't let him. A second later, he knew he could never hide behind Farber's unprofessional rigidity.

"Judge Smithers' wants me there." He hoped his honor would agree, in spirit, if asked, and he was certain Farber was never going to make that inquiry.

He didn't have to look at Farber's face to know his expression had softened. "That's different. If he wants you there, you've absolutely got to go."

Kenderson started toward the front door when the urge to phone Phil Hawkins one last time made him turn back to his office. He dialed, prepared to wait for the endless rings before hanging up. On the third ring, Phil answered. Kenderson felt like a ton had been removed from his back as he said: "I've been trying to reach you. Ivers said you were in Sacramento and couldn't be reached."

"The meeting was urgent and called at the last minute. What can I do for you?"

Kenderson hesitated. If Phil was involved in the plot to kill Freddie, he was about to put his ward at an even greater risk. "A guy by the name of Simstead suddenly showed up on D Unit and been assigned as a trustee to take care of Freddie. I'm afraid he's there to kill the boy."

There was a strained silence before Phil replied. "Curt Simstead is one of my brother, Pete's, cronies. I have no idea what he's doing there but somebody with clout arranged it. Don't worry about Simstead, I'll see that he doesn't harm Freddie."

Kenderson felt the tension drain out his body. He weighed telling Phil about the plot to escape from the courtroom, but decided against it. It didn't matter because Freddie no longer had to risk his life in a foolhardy escape attempt.

Kenderson's thanks to Phil Hawkins was heartfelt.

"I'll phone you when I've sorted this out." Phil said before he hung up.

Kenderson glanced at his watch and felt a moment of panic. It was five minutes to one and he must tell Freddie he would be safe at the Correctional Center, that Phil would guarantee his protection.

Hurrying out the door, he tried to comfort himself with the thought that judges are often late getting back from lunch. The Datsun was stubborn about starting and by the time he raced up the City Hall steps, it was eight minutes after one.

As he hurried to a seat behind Freddie, he could see that the session had already started. Goldstein was addressing Judge Smithers. The boy was sitting next to Ivers in a lightweight suit, without legs chains or cuffs. The two deputies standing behind Freddie looked bored. Kenderson leaned forward and whispered, "Freddie, cool it. Phil's back in town. You'll be safe. Don't run!"

Ivers glanced around, frowning. "What are you saying?"

Before he could answer, he heard Freddie's two quick coughs and watched helplessly as the boy whirled out of his seat, pushed though the swinging gate, and dashed up the aisle. Kenderson's response was automatic, sliding out of his seat and taking up the pursuit, shouting, "Freddie wait, don't run!" He could hear the deputies cursing and Judge Smithers shouting and gaveling for order. Three steps into the aisle, his right leg gave out and he slumped to the floor, tripping the foremost deputy, who crashed down on top of him. He could see the other one nearly trip over the sprawling legs of his partner.

As he rose to his knees, the deputies were racing through the courtroom doors. He slowly got to his feet, fighting the cramp in his leg. Ivers was standing next to him, asking, "What the hell's the matter with that idiot kid? Now he's got a new charge facing him. He must have been planning to run, and suckered me into asking the judge to let him sit without restraints."

Kenderson sat down heavily, his leg aching. He blamed himself for arriving too late to tell Freddie the news. He had a second thought. Had Freddie heard his message and decided to run anyway?

He watched as Ivers and Goldstein conferred with an angry Judge Smithers. Five minutes later, the two deputies came back to the courtroom looking irritated. "I'm sorry, your honor, the kid got away. We've put out an all points bulletin. We'd have got him if it wasn't for this guy taking a spill. They looked suspiciously at Kenderson, whose mind was racing. He felt he should apologize, and explain. "I'm his PO. Sorry, my leg gave out. It does that. Some shrapnel from Nam."

The tallest deputy shrugged. "We'll get his ass soon enough."

There was nothing more to do, so he limped out of the courtroom. As he started his Datsun, he felt a sudden uninvited elation. *I would have gotten away with it!*

For the moment, his ward was safe. But until Hawkins' killer was caught, ending the threat of in-court revelations and damaging publicity, the boy had to stay hidden. He drove slowly back to the office, dreading having to explain to Farber what had happened. That would be tough because he wasn't sure he really knew.

Freddie, breathing hard, hunkered down behind some oleander bushes in an alley three blocks from the Court House. He'd lay low until dark. The derelicts who sprawled in the shade of the empty buildings, nursing their wine bottles, hardly glanced at him. He thought, the Bar and Grill would be the first place the cops would look. Then Ermon's dump of a trailer. He decided against his Aunt Sarah's apartment because she'd fold up if the cops came to the door asking about him. So he'd end up where he intended to in the first place. Where nobody would think of looking.

He took off his coat and tie and, folding them into a makeshift pillow, burrowed deeper into the oleanders and fell asleep.

He awoke an hour later, feeling confused and hyper. Time for a Ritalin before he did something dumb. Around four o'clock, Freddie made a quick dash through the alley to MacCormick Park. He mingled with the shoppers who used the park paths to walk from one shopping mall to the other. No one seemed to notice him and leaving the park, he walked two more blocks and entered the sheltering limbs of a tall willow tree and peered out at the white bell tower of Santa Inglesia's First Presbyterian Church. Everything around the parking lot seemed quiet but his attention focused on the Earl Hawkins Education Building, a separate wooden structure named after his old man and used as a social hall and for Sunday morning classes for kids. He'd been one of them when his Mom was alive. He left the shelter of the tree and hurried to the front door.

He glanced over his shoulder before using the square of plastic to slip the lock. It was an easy job he'd done before. He quickly ducked inside and scrunched his body into one of the small chairs in the kindergarten classroom. He'd done plenty of time sitting on his ass on those seats when he was little. His stomach growled, reminding him he hadn't eaten any lunch.

There should be cookies or milk in the refrigerator, left over from some stupid meeting during the week or the coffee hour the previous Sunday. The milk and chocolate cookies were okay. He went back to one of the small chairs and piled the cookies and glass of milk in front of him on a matching table. He suddenly felt safe, remembering his mother leading him by the hand to the kindergarten class every Sunday before she went to the regular services. Afterward, on the way home, they'd stop for sundaes at some fancy ice cream place. He sighed. Stupid to think about something that was no more.

He glanced out the glass section of the door to make sure nobody was snooping around. From the past, he knew that one or two secretaries might be working in offices on the opposite side of the church.

He thought of phoning his Aunt Sarah and asking her to bring him some food for later. He decided not to, instead, looking around for a water faucet to take his Ritalin. He kept reminding himself to take the medication on schedule, to keep from doing something stupid and get locked up again, and maybe killed. It was going to be a long afternoon and night. If he was back in D Unit, he'd be on his sack sleeping like all the other dummies.

After his mother died and they'd named the annex after the old man, the elders had set aside the second floor for "The Honoree's" use as an office. Freddie remembered a couch and safe up there. Maybe the phone was still connected. He climbed the stairs. In the far corner, dusty cobwebs completely covered a stack of tattered hymnals and a small, ancient-looking metal safe. Whatever was in it, nobody had opened it for a long time.

He walked to the couch and threw a pile of torn choir robes on the floor and lay down, feeling drowsy. He closed his eyes, trying to relax. It didn't work. He was too pumped to sleep. He swung his feet over the side and looked around for the telephone. It sat on the floor close to the head of the stairs. He picked it up, listening for a dial tone. It worked. He grinned as he dialed his PO's number. The guy was okay, the way he hit the floor. It sure-assed slowed the deputies.

Kenderson sat in his office, weighing his next move. Tell Farber his ward had escaped? He knew the guy would flip, because it would be a black mark against his career. Start looking for Freddie? He hated the idea of driving in the afternoon sun without air conditioning. He was sure nobody would tell him where Freddie was, even if they'd seen him.

Nehi solved the problem as he walked through the front door, having just come from a class at MacCormick University. Kenderson beckoned to him and once the big man was seated, he closed the door.

"Freddie escaped from the courthouse about three hours ago. I was there and when I tried to catch up with him my leg gave out, tripping one of the deputies and slowing the second one." He thought of telling Nehi about the original plan, but decided to confine his comments to his suspicions about Simstead. He smiled in relief, telling Nehi about Phil Hawkins promising to protect his adoptive brother.

Nehi was silent for a few seconds before he spoke. "Did you fall down on purpose?"

Kenderson felt his face flush. Almost stammering, he said, "I admit I thought of it, but after Phil's promise to deal with Simstead, I told Freddie he had no reason to escape. But it was nearly ten after one by the time I got to the courthouse. I'm not sure he heard what I was saying."

Nehi shook his head. "Jay, you've got to get that boy to cooperate with you. If he's innocent, he can help with an alibi that will stand up. From what you're telling me, somebody wants him dead and he's acting like this is a Nintendo game."

The phone on his desk rang. He instantly recognized his ward's voice: "Freddie, where are you?"

Washington stood closer to the phone, nodded that he could hear. "You did good."

Kenderson's exasperation's came through. "You didn't have to run. Phil said he'd take care of Simstead. Didn't you hear what I said?"

"I heard, but I take care of me. Talk to you later." The dial tone buzzed in his ear. Washington raised an eyebrow.

"What are you going to do now?"

Dreading the thought of a Farber lecture, he said, "I'm going to the Elks Lodge and do some laps and treat my sore leg to some Jacuzzi time. Want to come?"

Washington shook his head. "Next time."

Because he worked on a flexible schedule and put in lots of overtime without pay, Kenderson felt okay about leaving the Diversion Center. Once at the Elks, he stripped, showered and did a half hour of laps, using his usual scissor and frog kick styles to strengthen the quadriceps muscles in his right knee. Afterward, he relaxed in the 104 degree Jacuzzi.

After a shower and shampoo, he quickly toweled off, feeling better. He stopped by the Diversion Office and picked up a phone message from Sarah MacCormick. He dialed her number and from the anxiety in her voice, he was sure she'd heard about Freddie's escape on the radio but, to his surprise, she didn't mention it. She wanted to talk about a phone call she'd just received.

"Harold Fisher, the detective I told you about, the one my father had hired before his murder, just phoned, saying he had some new information about Earl Hawkins' early years in Chicago. He said it might help you find the killer. He wanted money, but I told him I couldn't pay. He said something about blackmail video tapes Hawkins had made in the past few years, and he thought he knew where they were located. He urged me to raise some money and he'd get back to me."

Kenderson wondered if Fisher was a scam artist, trying to cash in on her hatred for Hawkins. Blackmail videos? Was the guy hinting the killer's face was on those tapes? He felt his heart pound. Whose transgressions had Hawkins recorded? Someone threatened enough to commit murder? Were the killer or killers looking for the tapes? Fisher must not know Sarah was broke and beholden to her brother-in-law. Obviously, he hadn't been in Santa Inglesia for years. Sarah interrupted his thoughts.

I'll phone and ask him to meet us at my place right now." Kenderson's first impulse was to refuse. The last thing he needed was to get mixed up with some fly-by-night con artist. But what if Fisher's story was true? So far he hadn't uncovered any local leads, so why not check the guy out.

"I'll be over right away."

He confirmed her address and on the way, used his portable phone to tell Fran he might be late getting home. "Phone you, hon, when I'm on my way."

Sarah MacCormick's shabby, one bedroom flat, must have been a terrible comedown for the attractive woman who had once lived in luxury, Kenderson thought. Fisher, a thin angular man, rose when Kenderson entered. His handshake was dry and brief.

"If Arnie Setich's goons find me in Santa Inglesia, I'm dead."

"Why do they want to kill you?" Kenderson hoped his voice didn't betray his increasing nervousness. Dealing with murder and blackmail had not been part of his schooling.

"They tried to kill me once before, but Pete botched the job and I escaped." Fisher's tone was strangely unemotional.

"Why did they want to kill you?" Kenderson decided he'd gone too far to back out now.

"It was Earl Hawkins' idea. I let him know I had the goods on him from Chicago. What's more, I discovered witnesses who would swear he was behind the Meadows rackets and murders. But he refused to pay me a dime.

"I got careless one night, and Pete slugged me and dumped me in the trunk of his car. Lucky for me, I was conscious when he opened the trunk. He was parked alongside the river and prepared to shoot me and dump me in the water. I hit him with a tire iron and took his car to the airport in the next county. I've been out of California for three years."

"Why come back now?"

"I figured with the Hawkins name in the headlines, the videos would be more marketable."

"Why not go to the police? Tell them about the tapes?"

"Cops don't pay for evidence. But someone will pay through the nose for these babies, and then I'll get the hell out of California for good."

"Where are the videos?"

"They're hidden in one of Hawkins' offices. A guy who worked on the safe told me he saw video tapes inside." Turning to Kenderson, he added, "The blackmail videos should tell you who wanted Hawkins dead."

He was suddenly all business. "I've recorded a forty-five minute videotape revealing the crimes, past and present, of the Hawkins organization.

"I'll send a copy to Arnie Setich, hoping he'll pay big money to keep it out of circulation. If he won't buy, I'll try to sell it to some talk show or national magazine. But if Arnie catches up to me, I'll be dead and gone. If I can't make money, I want those two to get a lot of prison time."

He handed Sarah a slip of paper. "Phone this number if you hear something's happened to me. They've been instructed to hand over my video tape to you."

After Fisher left, Sarah hid the slip of paper at the bottom of a brown cookie jar sitting on the counter. A moment later, the doorbell buzzer sounded. The apartment was on the second floor and Kenderson saw Sarah hesitate before answering the intercom. Reluctantly, she did. "Who's there?"

"It's me, Pete, and a buddy. We're looking for Freddie. He split from the courthouse this afternoon."

"Freddie's not here. I haven't seen him."

"Sarah, buzz us in. We're here on orders to find Freddie. And we won't leave until you let us in. Arnie says we're to search your place, period."

"Pete, I'm busy. Mr. Kenderson, Freddie's social worker, is here."

"So we'd like to talk to him, too, okay?"

Sarah looked at Kenderson, who nodded. A few moments later, Pete walked through the apartment door, followed by the man he'd seen at the Correctional Center.. Offhandedly, Pete introduced his companion. "This is an old buddy, Curt Simstead. He's helping me look for the kid."

Without stopping, they inspected the bedroom and closet. Kenderson could see Pete bending down to look under the bed. A quick look at the kitchen, and they were back facing Sarah and Kenderson.

"Just before we rang the bell, a guy looking like that asshole detective your old man hired years ago, took off down the street in a Rent-A-Wreck Toyota. So why was Fisher here? Is he trying to sell you the story there are video tapes which incriminate the old man? He's trying to peddle that story to anyone who'll listen."

Sarah's face was ashen. "He did say something like that. But I told him I have no money, so he left."

"Did he say where he was staying?"

She shook her head.

"If he contacts you again, get an address, okay?"

Pete turned to Kenderson with a knowing grin. "So, did you help the kid split? Heard you fell down and held up the two deputies."

Kenderson shook his head. He was about to explain why he fell but suddenly thought, what the hell, they don't want to hear my excuses.

"Do you know where the kid is hiding?" Pete asked.

"No, I don't, but I'll be looking for him."

Simstead edged a little closer to Kenderson. "Be sure you do. We need to find the kid real bad."

Kenderson felt sudden rage. So you can kill him. Fuck you, you'll never find out from me. Aloud he said, "No idea where he's hiding."

Simstead faked a friendly smile, "You'll let us know, right?

Kenderson nodded again, hoping they'd leave before he made matters worse.

On the way out, Pete reminded Sarah about letting him know Fisher's address. She merely nodded as they walked out the door.

When he was sure they were out of earshot, Kenderson, asked, "Any idea where I should look for Freddie?"

She shook her head nervously. "I'm so upset now, I can't think. Later, if I remember something I'll phone you. About Fisher, what should I do?"

"I wouldn't do anything now. Wait until he contacts you again."

WEDNESDAY LATE AFTERNOON

He drove back to the Diversion Center to find two single mothers in his office. They had sons in his caseload and both were anxious because neither boy had shown up for school that day.

He gave them his usual advice. "If they're not home tonight, call the police and report them as runaways."

Two months earlier, they would have been shocked at the idea. Now they accepted the necessity of the boys facing consequences. After they left, he reflected that he should practice what he preached. Earl Hawkins had allowed Freddie to do what he pleased, and reaped the public's sympathy for putting up with an incorrigible son. Washington's last remark stuck in his mind. Insist that Freddie tell you where he was during the time period Earl Hawkins was killed.

Engrossed in writing updates in the weekly progress report, he delayed until the fourth ring to pick up the phone.

The anxious voice of Sarah MacCormick broke his concentration. "Freddie's here. He didn't want me to phone but I'm worried. When I told him about Harold Fisher telling us where he thinks the video tapes were hidden, Freddie said when he was a kid hanging out at the Front Street office, there *was* a safe where important stuff was stashed."

Kenderson suddenly heard Sarah's door crash open, followed by her scream and the thump of the phone hitting the floor. He heard the terror in her voice. "I don't know what either of you are talking about. Like I told you, I haven't seen Freddie."

He recognized the next voice as Simstead's."Okay, lady, you had your chance to do it the easy way. Now it gets harder. Let's go."

It sounded like she was being dragged. Her screaming suddenly stopped, the dragging sound fading. Before the door slammed shut, he heard Setich's voice. "Keep an eye on the apartment, Curt. The kid's bound to show up."

Kenderson cut the connection and dialed 911, giving the operator Sarah MacCormick's address. "I heard the assault and kidnaping over the phone, please hurry." He gave his name and phone number, weighing whether to name her assailants. If the Hawkins organization had the dispatchers on their payroll, naming Setich would make sure the call would be buried.

The phone nearly slipped out of his sweating hand before he could cradle it. His face felt on fire and his heart thumps beat in his ears. What kind of crazy world have I stepped into? He thought of phoning Washington but suddenly, the phone rang. It was Freddie.

"I'm at my aunt's. They took her. Simstead is watching the place. They were out front but I used an old ladder to make it through the back bathroom window and hid when they came looking for me. Now someone is watching the back. I'm stuck."

"How are you going to get out of there? Should I come over?"

"Man, no way. Phone Ermon. Tell him to drive his clunker by my aunt's house in about fifteen minutes."

"Where will you go when you get out?"

"I'll phone if I make it."

"Freddie, wait." But hearing the dial tone, he hung up. His life was getting messier by the minute. Who could he trust? Only Phil had come through for him. He dialed the number but after an eternity of rings, no voice mail message came on.

Minutes later he dialed Ermon's number. His mother answered, sounding drunk. When he identified himself, she screamed: "You let that Freddie bastard ruin my boy!" Ignoring her tirade, he continued asking for Ermon. He could hear the boy arguing with his mother, and finally his voice on the phone. He repeated Freddie's instructions. To Kenderson's surprise, the boy's response was simply,"I'm on my way, man."

Freddie peered in his aunt's clothes closet. Simstead would be watching for a young guy wearing a suit, not a woman in her mid-thirties. He held up skirts and blouses. Shit, he'd never get in those threads. He decided to wait until the last minute before changing clothes. But sitting on his ass was killing him. He'd better check outside. Too early for Ermon but maybe he could spot Simstead's car. Being careful not to show himself in front of the windows, he edged to the wall facing Park Street. Pulling back the curtain, he stared out. The blue Chevy van across the street looked familiar. One of Pete's? Far down the street, he spotted the beat-up Datsun, barely visible behind a Santa Inglesia Utility Truck. What the hell's my PO doing? Is he going to take on Simstead? The thought made Freddie laugh.

He couldn't see anyone behind the van's wheel. Simstead must be ducking down or hiding in the rear.

Hurrying to the bedroom, he opened the sliding door to the closet and grabbed a skirt with a plaid pattern. He picked up a faded blue sweater from the top shelf and, taking off his shirt and pants, he managed to force the sweater over his head. It bound under his arm pits. The skirt was too tight to fasten the metal snaps. He searched deeper into the closet depths. Jerking a brown, full-length coat with a fur collar off the hanger, he wrapped it around his shoulders. A full length mirror caught his reflection. Who in the hell would he fool? Wearing a coat on a warm afternoon? He knew the skirt and sweater alone wouldn't work.

Maybe Simstead wouldn't pay close attention to a woman walking out. But he couldn't take a chance. Sweeping three round hat boxes off the shelf, he found a brown wig perched on a Styrofoam head. At his first try, the hairpiece covered his face and eyes. He jerked it off and turned it around. He could at least see. Shit, anyone looking at him close would know he was a phony. He decided his regular shoes would have to do. No way was he going to try to get his feet into his aunt's footwear. He might have to run like hell.

Crouching low, he hurried back to the window and parted the curtain. The van hadn't moved. Where was that fucking Ermon? He would have to spot the clunker before it stopped in front. Then run like hell down a flight of stairs, out to the street, and pile inside before Simstead caught on. Knowing he'd be without food, he hurried to the kitchen and grabbed the last three slices of bread and stuffed them in the pocket of the brown coat. As an after-thought, he took a pint carton of orange juice and stuck it in the other pocket, then decided he wouldn't have to run so far if he waited in the lobby downstairs.

After glancing up and down the narrow hallway, he hurried down the one flight and opened the outside door enough to see a car coming.

He let out his breath when he saw the wheezing Dodge pull up and double park across from the apartment. The stupid bastard had come in the wrong way! He fought down an urge to throw off the coat and run to the car. Be cool. No use screwing up his disguise. Steeling himself, he pushed open the right wing of the double door and walked down the stairs to the sidewalk. He could see Ermon peering around, looking for him. The asshole. It wasn't until he was almost to the car that Ermon saw him. "Jesus, Freddie is that you?" Hoping to save time by entering the back seat, Freddie jerked at the sticking left rear door and after tugging like hell, opened it, got in and sat on top an oily wrench and jack handle before crouching down low. "Get the fuck out of here! Stay on Park!"

"Hey, man, I'd never knowed it was you. Some outfit." Freddie wanted to slug Ermon with the jack handle but controlled his voice. "Don't speed, just go. I'll tell you when to turn." When he let in the clutch, the Dodge jerked and rocked until he'd ground it into second. Glancing out the rear window, Freddie saw a trail of black smoke boiling from the broken exhaust pipe. As they passed the blue van, he saw a figure slumped down on the passenger side. It was Simstead. Freddie hoped the guy was asleep and hadn't noticed him. Just after they passed, the right door opened and Simstead stood for a moment looking at the retreating car, then hurried around to the driver's side.

Get moving, Ermon. He's spotted us." He could tell Ermon was rattled. He was driving all over the goddamned street.

Turn left on Silver! You're about there."

For a moment, Freddie considered diving out of the car when it slowed, and hiding behind one of the hedges in front of homes on either side of the street. Glancing back, he saw his PO's Datsun pull away from the curb and make a U turn in the middle of the street. Oh man, I hope he can slow down the van which was starting to follow.

Give her hell, man," Freddie shouted. "Turn left when you get to Monroe, and then give these guys a chase for as long as you can. I'm heading for that shed in back of the Bar and Grill. Be in touch." No way could he tell Ermon his real destination. The first time Simstead stuck a gun in Ermon's face, the fat boy would spill his guts.

Silver Street dead ended at Monroe and was in direct line with the hedge and fence which ran along the rear of the First Presbyterian Church parking area. He could see Monroe coming up fast. It didn't really matter at which section of the hedge he bailed out because he could crawl out of sight in a matter of seconds.

Looking back, he saw the Datsun poking along and the van tailgating behind. It was time to make his move.

"When you get on Monroe, move into the right lane and slow down. I'll bail out. Remember, I'll be in back of the B and G. If they catch up with you, don't tell Simstead where I'm holed up, okay?"

As they approached the busy thoroughfare Freddie raised his head, watching heavy traffic moving both ways. Ermon began to slow for the red stop light. "Fuck stopping man, get the hell across the street!"

The heavy car rushed through the red light and Freddie could hear tires squealing and shouting. A Nissan pickup bounced off the left front fender, crushing it as Ermon fought to make the left hand turn. Cars on the North-bound lane swerved wildly to avoid being hit broadside by the runaway Dodge. Ermon finally maneuvered near the right hand curb and in a flash, Freddie slid from the rear seat and dived for the protection of the thick hedge. He felt the orange juice carton fly from his coat pocket and heard it splash in the gutter. He glanced out, hopeful that neither his PO nor Simstead had spotted him. Safely out of sight, scrunched under the heavy foliage, the loud hollering and cussing on the street made him laugh.

He heard Ermon grinding gears, trying to get thc hcll away from the bent fenders, busted bumpers and highly pissed off drivers. Turned out perfect! The cops would probably catch Ermon before Simstead did. He'd get his ass booked in juvie. No big deal, he'd been there before. The Dodge's rumbling engine faded. Good, he'd made it and if Simstead had gotten through the mess of cars, it would take time to catch up with Ermon.

Kenderson heard the banging of metal against metal before he reached the stop light on Monroe. He'd done his best to slow the blue van, obviously in pursuit of Ermon's ancient Dodge. Cars were scattered all over Monroe Boulevard, stopping traffic in both directions. My God, he thought, now I'm an accessory to a traffic disaster. He felt some relief seeing most of the pileups were fender benders. Sirens approached and as he watched, a patrol car stopped in the middle of the street and two officers began approaching the gridlocked cars. He glanced behind, expecting to find the blue van and an angry Curt Simstead glowering at him. To his surprise, the van was nowhere in sight.

Freddie put the brown coat to one side, after having used it as a cushion on the hard ground. The wig hung over a small branch. All he had to do now was to be cool and wait. He figured it was almost an hour before cars started passing without stopping. In that time, he counted four tow trucks and at least seven black and whites on the scene. He laughed, listening to drivers trying to explain to the traffic cops what caused the big mess. They plain didn't know. He and Ermon were in the clear. And the cops wouldn't have any idea where to start looking for him. Neat!

Freddie needed to piss but was afraid he'd wet himself if he tried. Time to find the hole in the chain link fence. He stuck the wig back on his head and got back on the street. He'd only be in sight for a minute until he found the fence opening. A quick ducking back inside the hedge and be out of sight. His legs felt cramped when he started walking and the goddamned skirt had hiked way up and twisted around his ass. He left the coat. He'd find some other clothes. No way he was going to keep wearing that silly looking stuff. He felt good. He was living on the freaking edge, the way he liked to. The opening in the fence was near Fredrick. Two teen-age girls were coming his way. He didn't want any shit out of them and quickly turned his head like he was interested in the hedge. It didn't work. "Woo-e.e.," he heard one of them laugh, "Cool threads." To Freddie's relief they kept going still giggling down the block.

Once again he would have to disappear in broad daylight. Without glancing in either direction he squatted low and dove head-first into the narrow opening. Sharp branches jabbed into his head and neck. For sweaty seconds he listened for shouts he'd been seen. He waited for a full minute and then breathed easier. He felt like laughing. He'd made it again! Perfect! He took more punishment from the branches as he squirmed around to face the fence. The jagged gap lay five feet in front of him. He wriggled through the hole into the empty parking lot and staying close to the Fredrick Street fence, moved toward the annex. Once there he used his plastic card again on the simple lock and edged inside, quickly closing the door.

The first thing he needed was to piss and headed for the boy's toilet. His aunt's skirt had twisted so bad he could hardly walk. The tight sweater bound his armpits. What was worse, he'd have to walk through the Meadows in that freaky outfit. No way. He'd be mugged or raped before he'd gone a block. Somehow he had to get different clothes.

He wondered if his old man ever kept changes in his bogus office. They wouldn't fit but it would be better than his aunt's rags. It didn't surprise Freddie to find a tuxedo, white shirt and black tie encased in a plastic cover. Rolling up the pants cuffs worked okay and the white shirt didn't look too baggy.

Easing out the side door he skirted the rear of the annex, around the main building and keeping close to the chain-link fence next to Bryner he waited. Traffic was slow, and hurrying to Eighth Street he turned east and ducked quickly into the narrow alley between Bryner and Madeline streets. It was familiar territory. Walking between the stretches of sagging backyard fences and beat-up buildings on either side of the alley, Freddie felt safe knowing cops seldom cruised this asshole part of Santa Inglesia.

He realized he was hungry. It was a temptation to go by the Seven-Eleven on Seventh and Filloy to buy a chili dog and a coke. Too risky. He kept looking for a phone booth to call Ermon and maybe his PO. He decided Kenderson was in too deep to turn him down now.

Seeing the fender benders on Monroe, Kenderson made a U turn and headed back to Sarah MacCormick's apartment. He hoped Pete and Setich merely wanted to scare her and failing to locate Freddie, would let her go. He parked and hurrying up the steps to the front door, punched the button above her apartment number. He buzzed several times then hurried back to the car and dialed the non-emergency police number of his portable phone.

"My name is Kenderson, and I phoned 911 about a half hour ago to report an assault and kidnaping of a Sarah MacCormick from her apartment. Has she been found?"

A business-like female voice responded: "Let me check our computer. Please hold." Kenderson felt his heart race as the delay stretched on. What is she doing? The information on the police computers should be the same as those on those recorded in the 911 Center. Why the delay?

The same voice, this time tinged with uncertainty, came back on the line. "Are you sure you made the call? There is nothing recorded on the police computer or in the Emergency Center about an assault or kidnaping. Are you sure you reported this correctly? And what was your name again?"

Kenderson's felt sick. Was it any use? Setich obviously had the vital police emergency network under his control. He wondered if the Sheriff's Department was in Setich's pocket, too. Maybe not. He'd read about jurisdictional rivalry between the two departments. "Officer, here is what I reported, can you make sure this information gets to the Sheriff's Office immediately." He quickly repeated the details of Sarah's assault and kidnaping. "And my name is Nate Farber, Director of the Juvenile Diversion Center." He pushed the red END button.

He keyed Phil Hawkins' number into the portable and waited. He felt his anger grow as the ringing continued. This man was two months from an election and he couldn't afford to pay someone to answer the phone? Why in hell wasn't his voice mail working? It didn't make sense.

His thoughts turned to Freddie. Where was he hiding? It was time to get some straight answers.

He punched in the office number and told Marilyn he'd be gone for the rest of the day. "If Freddie Hawkins phones, give him my portable number."

Mr. Farber told me not to take any more of Freddie's calls."

He felt like cussing but restrained himself. "Please, this is a real emergency. I'll explain it to Mr. Farber. You won't get into trouble."

She sounded doubtful but agreed.

He called Ermon's number and after listening to the usual hassle with the mother, the boy came on the line. His voice shook.

That guy in the van caught me. He said he'd shoot me if I didn't tell where Freddie was hiding." Ermon sounded like he was crying. "Put a gun up to my head. I didn't want to be dead."

"So where is Freddie?"

"In the shed behind the Bar and Grill."

Kenderson felt sick. He pictured Freddie lying in a pool of blood amid the weeds and rusting car parts back of the ghetto bar. Maybe not. Kenderson guessed Freddie would never trust Ermon with the truth. "Ermon, stay out of sight, okay?" He punched END. Simstead, Setich's goon, would be looking for Ermon if he didn't find Freddie.

He felt frustrated at the thought of phoning Phil. Did the man know when he was calling and deliberately refuse to answer? Kenderson knew call blocking made that possible. In any case, he must find Freddie.

He thought of dialing his office but realized it was after five o'clock and Marilyn had gone for the day. He started the Datsun and headed for the Bar and Grill. Maybe the boy was hanging out near there. Three blocks later, the phone buzzed and he flipped it on.

"Man, I need help." Freddie's scared voice mercifully ended the nightmare he had been imagining.

"You're okay? Where are you? I'm heading for the Bar and Grill."

"Turn right on Filloy. I'll be watching for you."

Pablo Gomez, one of the boys on his caseload, lived on that shanty town street. He slowed down, looking carefully to the right and left. Approaching a stand of bamboo bushes on a vacant lot, he shifted to a lower gear. It was a logical hiding place. Nothing. He drove on past several ragged looking children playing in the streets. Reaching the dead end, he turned and started back. Had he heard Freddie right? It was Filloy. As he neared the bamboo patch, Freddie darted out to the car. To Kenderson's astonishment, he was dressed in an oversize white shirt and black, rolled-up tuxedo pants. He jumped in the passenger seat and ducked down. "Wanted to see if you were being followed."

He's wiser than I am, Kenderson thought. What next? Only one option seemed possible. Take Freddie home and somehow persuade Fran to provide the boy with a temporary shelter and hiding place, and some suitable clothes. Sighing deeply, he knew she would hate it.

Freddie kept a rapid-fire account of what had happened, hardly pausing for breath. His rapid speech pattern, a familiar ADHD symptom, caused Kenderson to ask if the boy had his Ritalin with him.

"I'm running low. I made sure I kept close to my regular hours during court and afterward. I was afraid if I forgot, my head would start tripping and I'd do something stupid and get caught."

"Okay, calm down. We're going to my house to get you some clothes to wear. We'll figure out what to do then."

Freddie continued his irritating speech until they turned into Fehr Court, where Kenderson lived. "Okay, duck down and keep quiet."

Turning into the driveway, he punched the remote garage door opener and parked next to Fran's Plymouth. First thing he had to do was get some Ritalin into Freddie before the boy drove everyone nuts. He led Freddie through the door leading into the kitchen and thumbed the button which closed the garage door.

Hastening to the cupboard, he took down a glass and filled it with water at the sink. "Give me your Ritalin bottle, please." The boy's hand dived into the deep tux pockets and Kenderson held his breath, fearing the prescription had been lost. After a tense few seconds, Freddie's hand emerged holding the round prescription bottle. Examining the contents, Kenderson saw that there was barely enough for one more day. Ritalin's effect lasted no longer than four hours. He guessed there were six left. With relief, he watched Freddie down one of the pills. In a few minutes, he'd be down off his high. Glancing at the battery operated clock over the door to the garage, he saw it was just five thirty. Where were Fran and the kids? Glancing out the sliding glass doors, he saw her sitting on the patio, reading at the circular table shaded by the white roll up canopy. The kids were slowly tossing a tennis ball to Bandit, their aged, but still sprightly cat, who cuffed it with her front paws.

Was he right in bringing Freddie into his own home? Wasn't he jeopardizing his own family? He suddenly realized there was no need for Cindy and Vernon to know about Freddie. But he must bring Fran up to date on the dangerous mess linking his fate to Freddie Hawkins. He escorted Freddie back to the office, telling him to wait quietly. He closed the door, walked back to the front room and slid the glass door open.

Fran smiled when he called out to her. "No late appointments?" He shook his head. "Need to talk to you, hon. It's important."

She put the book down and slowly rose to her feet. After all their years of marriage, he still admired her slim good looks and the graceful way she moved her body.

He took her hand and led her back to their bedroom and closed the door. She raised her eyebrows and laughed, "Important business?"

"Please sit down, hon. Freddie Hawkins is in the office." Fran's smile vanished. "Freddie Hawkins! What's he doing in my home?"

"Earl Hawkins' men are trying to murder him! Was there any news about his escaping from the courtroom this afternoon?" She shook her head. "Nothing like that!" Fran was an inveterate radio listener when home alone. He felt a shiver of fear run down his spine. If news of a escape from a county courtroom could be suppressed, the Hawkins/Setich's corruption network had to include the County Sheriff's and DA's office.

Talking fast, Kenderson told an astonished Fran about reporting to 911, Sarah MacCormick's forced removal from her apartment, only to learn later there was no record of his call. He hurriedly described Simstead's sinister appearance at the jail and the plan to help Freddie escape from the courtroom. Fran looked stricken.

"What's happening to you? You could go to jail and lose your license and....get killed." Her eyes began to tear. He held her for a moment.

"Phil Hawkins assured me he would protect Freddie but I got to court late and he ran before I could stop him. I tried to reach Phil again but there was no answer."

Kenderson knew what was coming next. Fran worked three half days for the DA's office and believed her boss could do no wrong.

"Mr. Fabretti would never stand for any of this. Why didn't you tell him what was going on?"

Robert White

Earl Hawkins backed Fabretti in the last elections. And Jerry Goldstein was in court when Freddie ran out. Why wouldn't he give that information to the *Sentinel* reporters or the TV and radio stations? He normally would, unless he was told to keep the escape quiet. I don't think either of us can assure Freddie that your boss wouldn't turn him over to Arnie Setich to be killed."

He could see the doubt growing on her face. "My God, if what you say is true, this is some kind of a nightmare. Who can be trusted?

"Ourselves, the Washingtons, and probably a lot of decent people we don't even know. My gut feeling is Sergeant Castro, Al Fallon and the rest of the squad aren't on Hawkins' payroll."

"Castro's sure Freddie killed Earl Hawkins, isn't he? Why are you so sure he didn't?"

"A hunch. Something inside the boy makes him stop before he goes too far."

Kenderson felt on edge. He had to find clothes and get Freddie out of his home. He guessed that Vernon and Freddie were about the same size. Fran left the bedroom, to return immediately with jeans and a sport shirt of Vernon's.

"Stay in here while I get him dressed and out of here. If anyone asks, you haven't seen Freddie Hawkins."

"Where will you take him?"

"Don't ask. He won't even tell me. Can you make up a couple of sandwiches and include a pint of milk?"

Fran hurried out to the kitchen, and a moment later he heard her opening the refrigerator. When he went to the office, Freddie was hunched over the computer keyboard. "Put these on quick. Can you take the stuff you're wearing back where you found it." Freddie nodded.

"Okay, I'm going to get my family out of the way, and then you and I will leave. You say you have a good hiding place. Will you be safe for the night?" Freddie nodded."Stay here. I'll be back."

When he returned to the kitchen, he saw Vernon and Cindy were still in the backyard. He motioned Fran to return to the patio, and then went back for his ward.

A deep, foreboding shook him. His family must be able to truthfully say they hadn't seen Freddie Hawkins. He led Freddie, now dressed in jeans and T shirt, through the door to the garage and opened the Datsun's back door.

"Stay down, and where do you want me to drop you?"

"Where you picked me up on Filloy."

"You're sure?"

On the run to the Meadows, Freddie began to talk about the video tapes Fisher had mentioned. "Man, I think they're hidden in the safe on Front Street. If we could get hold of them, we'd know who the old bastard was squeezing."

"And who might have wanted him dead," Kenderson added, but he was too tense to concentrate on video tapes at the moment. "Let's get you safe first."

Before turning on Filloy, Kenderson handed Freddie a brown bag with the sandwiches and milk. "Will you need my portable phone?"

"I've got one I can use."

"You'll need your Ritalin. I've put the remainder in the bag but I'll keep the bottle to get the prescription renewed."

As they passed the grove of bamboo, Kenderson slowed and heard the rear door open and close. He didn't look in that direction until he'd U-turned and was driving East. He was relieved to see Freddie had disappeared.

Driving back to his home, the assault on Sarah MacCormick burned in his mind. Had this happened because

Setich thought she knew where Freddie was hiding? Or did they fear she'd reveal some damaging information they suspected she'd overheard?

He was about to call Castro's number on his portable when it dawned on him that his phone's radio frequency might not be secure. Stopping at the Seven-Eleven Convenience Store, he walked over to the outside phone booth. He dialed the non-emergency police number and, to his surprise, Sergeant Castro answered.

"I've got to talk to you right away. Freddie ran away from court this afternoon. Did you know that?"

Sounding stunned, Castro said: "He escaped? You putting me on?"

"Then you didn't know? Can you meet me somewhere right away. Something terribly wrong is going on."

"I'm just leaving the station. Where are you now?"

Kenderson gave him the street number of the Seven-Eleven. "That's not far, I'm bringing Fallon."

WEDNESDAY EVENING

While waiting, Kenderson dialed his home and told Fran he'd be home later than usual. She started to ask about Freddie but he cut her off. "The package was delivered. We'll talk when I get home." He replaced the phone. Fran had sounded scared, which triggered his automatic self-blame routine. He told himself it was too late for recriminations. He'd done what he'd done and there was no turning back now.

The Sergeant was driving a Honda Accord with no police markings. Kenderson assumed it was his own car. He pulled up alongside the Datsun and saw Al Fallon in back. "Get in and we'll drive around," Castro ordered. Staying on the back streets of the Meadows driving slowly, both detectives listened intently as Kenderson related the day's events, including Simstead's suddenly showing up at the County Correctional Center as a trustee.

"No way that's going to happen unless somebody at the top orders it."

Kenderson looked at the wiry Hispanic and hoped his hunch was right. Castro returned the look."My name is Raul, so you don't have to keep calling me Sergeant. Next, why do you think me and my squad aren't on Arnie Setich's payroll?"

Kenderson weighed a polite answer but it didn't come out that way. "I guess because you're so goddamned stubborn and ornery." Castro laughed and Fallon joined in. "And I've been a sergeant for a hell of a long time. It's some of the lieutenants, captains and the administrators who are in on this. It's not the first time I've seen this kind of bullshit happen." He paused after a moment's thought. "Why are they trying to kill the kid? Why not let some con in prison do the job?

"I don't know. When I mention Setich, he panics. Swears he'd never reveal anything on the witness stand. It's almost like he wants me to phone Arnie Setich and put in a good word for him."

"Then he knows something they don't want broadcast."

Kenderson nodded. "Within the past year, the old man sent him to the Meadows with Arnie and Pete. That's what Sarah MacCormick told me. And that's another weird happening." He told Castro how his emergency call had never been recorded. "Is there anything you can do to find her?"

Fallon suddenly spoke and the anger in his voice was unmistakable. "Those bastards took Sarah?"

"I heard her screaming, I felt so damned helpless."

Fallon spoke again, "Boss, let me handle this one. I knew Sarah as a kid. My old man was their gardener.

Castro turned in the seat. "Are you too close to be objective?"

"No way. But I won't rest until she's safe."

Looking at Kenderson, he said, "We'll talk later about what you know, okay?"

Kenderson suddenly felt better. Fallon struck him as a competent and determined ally. Fallon took over.

"Back to Freddie. Do you think he might have seen a killing? They happen often enough in the Meadows."

"And the cops just watch?"

Robert White

Both men bristled. Fallon said, "The cops assigned solely to the Meadows beat don't act like cops. The rest of us are told to ignore those calls."

Kenderson weighed telling the two detectives about Harold Fisher and the blackmail tapes he was after. He decided it was too late to hold back. He related what he'd learned from his meeting with Fisher. Castro said, "Al, you take over and I'll listen."

"Freddie thinks the videos are located at the Front Street office. It's such an isolated place, they could be holding Sarah MacCormick there, too. If those videos exist, there are others with a motive to kill Earl Hawkins.

"Maybe, maybe not." Fallon said, and Kenderson felt his face flush. Why was the guy such a bullheaded prick? He cooled off a moment later recognizing he, Kenderson, was the one who'd allowed Freddie to treat the homicide charge like a game. The boy's accounting for the time Earl Hawkins died was overdue.

"So, want to tell me where the kid is hiding?"

"I don't know and I don't I want to."

Fallon nodded. "Fair enough. We'd have to bring him in."

Castro drove his Honda back to the Seven-eleven. Before he got out of the car, Kenderson urged, "Sarah MacCormick may be in terrible danger."

Castro nodded. "This is your ball game, Al. Don't fuck it up." He looked directly at Kenderson. "We never had this drive or conversation, understand?"

As Kenderson finished parking the Datsun next to her Plymouth, Fran came out to meet him. She punched the button on the side of the entrance door to close the garage. Still standing on the bottom step, she said, "Let's talk here, away from the kids. Honey, I can't believe what's happening. Suddenly I'm faced with stories about corrupt police, kidnapings and death threats, and my own boss a suspected pawn of Earl Hawkins' criminal organization. From the moment you told everyone Freddie Hawkins didn't bash his adoptive father's head in, our world has become a nightmare. I feel we're all in terrible danger."

"I never intended this to happen. I'm scared, too. Honey, maybe you and the kids should go to your mother's in Walnut Creek."

Fran looked dazed and began shaking her head. "I can't run out on you. Maybe the kids should go." She stopped talking, then blurted, "Shit, I don't know what to do. I need time to think."

"I think I found someone who will help us. I told Sergeant Castro and Al Fallon, his top detective, everything I told you. I believe they're on the up and up. He said certain cops who are paid to ignore the extortion and violence are assigned to the Meadows. The others, like Castro and his squad, are forbidden to respond to police calls from that area." Kenderson shook his head. "When I left, they said they'd deny we ever talked."

"Then Hawkins had two organizations. The good citizen realtor and the ghetto crime boss. People never put the two together."

"It's starting to come out. Setich must be afraid Freddie and Sarah MacCormick might talk, now the big boss is dead."

"Oh, God, will they kill that poor woman?"

"I think not. They need to find out what she knows about a secret expansion project, and who she's talked to. Harold Fisher believes Hawkins invited some prominent Santa Inglesians to LA and then doped them and had camcorders record their evening with prostitutes. Those victims would have motives for murdering the man. Freddie thinks the tapes are at the Front Street Office. I went there but never got inside. It's isolated and strange. There's no way for the public to approach, except on foot. I can't help thinking they might be holding Sarah there."

"Did you tell the detectives?"

"Yes, but Front Street is next to the river and probably off limits for them."

"Oh, that's wonderful!" Fran struggled to control tears. "Can't anyone do anything? What about the state?"

"We both know state police guard state buildings. The Highway Patrol, except in emergencies, is confined to highway traffic problems. The Attorney General's office in Sacramento is a possibility, but I'm afraid an investigation would take weeks."

"Didn't you tell me Phil Hawkins promised to protect Freddie?"

"Yes, but he has an unlisted home phone. I can try to leave a message on his office phone, but half the time his answering machine isn't even on."

Fran began sobbing. Kenderson put his arm around her. "We need help." She stepped down to his level and put her head on his chest.

Before he was aware, Kenderson began silently berating himself for the awful mess he'd created. Fran and the kids should get out of town. He wished there was an out for him, but he was ethically bound to stand by Freddie Hawkins.

Fran dried her tears and, taking his hand, opened the door and led him into the kitchen. "Stop blaming yourself."

She knows me like a book, Kenderson thought.

Removing the wall phone, he shook his head and replaced it. "Cindy is on another marathon conversation on our line. Vernon must be hogging theirs."

"I'll ask her to get off." Fran left.

Reaching for the phone to try again to reach Phil Hawkins, it rang. Was Cindy's friend calling back? It was Al Fallon. "Who knows the layout of the Front Street office?"

"This guy Fisher and Freddie Hawkins."

"The screw up kid? Can he be trusted?"

He felt his anger rising, "Yes, when he's on his meds he's okay."

"If you say so. If not, it's my ass."

"Mine, too. I'll be along."

"Let's meet at the rear of the Seven-Eleven. Twenty minutes?"

Kenderson felt a surge of hope as he replaced the phone. He called to Fran and told her who'd just called.

"Do you want me to go with you?"

"Might spook the detective. Go ahead and feed the kids. I'll get something later.

A dark, late model Ford was parked at the side and rear of the Seven-Eleven. The first outside lights had just come on but enough daylight remained for Kenderson to recognize Fallon behind the wheel. He parked and waited The driver's side door opened and Fallon emerged. Kenderson spoke. "You want to talk in my car? I'll drive."

Fallon got in the passenger side and Kenderson backed out and drove slowly down the shabby street. Fallon spoke quickly. "Give you a little history. My Dad worked for the MacCormick family. I helped him after I graduated from high school. Sarah MacCormick was a friend of mine. We never dated, but we liked each other. I used to think her accusing Hawkins of murdering her father and sister was grief talking. When I got on the force and saw what was going on behind the scenes, I knew she'd been telling the truth. "I can't act officially, it'll have to be on my own."

Kenderson drove back to the Seven-Eleven and parked next to Fallon's car. Fallon handed Kenderson a slip of paper. Use this number when you need me. It's my beeper."

Fallon was getting into his car when Kenderson's cellular buzzed. He signaled Fallon to wait. Freddie sounded breathless.

"I'm calling from a phone booth on MacCormick two blocks from Front Street. There's nobody at the office. I need help getting in. They got padlocks on every door. Bring a crowbar and we can snatch those videos."

"Where will you be?"

"On the river side of Front."

"I'll be there in ten minutes."

Kenderson beckoned to Fallon, who hurried to the driver's side of the Datsun. "Freddie Hawkins just phoned." He explained what the boy wanted.

Fallon grinned. "I've got a crowbar, bolt cutters and two flashlights in the trunk. We'll use my car, okay?"

Grabbing his portable phone, Kenderson climbed into the passenger seat. The detective backed up and after leaving the parking lot, headed south.

"We won't be so conspicuous if you park on MacCormick Street with the other cars from that corner apartment. We'll walk from Second to First then to Front Street. Three short blocks. It's easier than struggling with the barricade. Besides, we don't want to be caught in that cul-de-sac."

"You've been there?"

Outside. It's a strange place. Built like a fort."

As the late summer twilight deepened, Kenderson, carrying the bolt cutter and a flashlight, led the way for Fallon, who had the crowbar and the other flash. Seeing the building sitting alone in the middle of the empty lots, Fallon grunted: "Weird is right."

Kenderson looked at the dark shadows of the oleanders for a sign of Freddie. He shone his light at the bushes. An instant later, Freddie's agitated voice. "Douse the lights."

Fallon grunted a greeting when Kenderson introduced Freddie. The boy ignored Fallon and led the two men to a side door on the opposite side of the building. Kenderson's light revealed a heavy padlock holding a thick, hinged hasp. The door surface was some kind of metal.

"You were right about a fort." Fallon said.

Freddie's words sounded strained. "The tapes have gotta be in there."

Listening to what he feared was just the start of Freddie's pressured speech, Kenderson knew they had to get the job done fast so he could get to a late-night drug store. "How did you get clear across town?"

"My boy, Ermon, picked me up but I sent him home. I'll need a ride."

"Okay, stay cool. We'll get in."

Illuminating the padlock, Kenderson watched Fallon work the bolt cutter blades over the padlock prongs and press down. Sweat glistened on the detective's face as he struggled to cut through. It took ten minutes before the padlock separated, and another five to break the other lock with the crowbar. Once inside, Kenderson stared in amazement. The lower floor was decorated like a brothel. Red quilts and pillows made satin mounds on a king-sized bed. The roving flashlight reflected on ceiling mirrors.

"Some realty office," Fallon laughed. "Old man Hawkins, the king of virtue, had himself a great spot here."

Kenderson shone the light slowly around the room but he could see nothing but heavy drapery. Turning to Freddie, who was agitatedly roaming the room, he said. "Is there a back door or a door that leads down to a basement?"

Robert White

The boy seemed so out of control, Kenderson physically stopped him. "Did you hear me? Is there another door down here. Think."

"The safe is upstairs--I need to find it."

"Okay, but let's look for the door first!"

Fallon was knocking on the wall at the rear of the room when he suddenly called out, "Quiet, I think I hear a voice. It's somewhere behind this section of the wall."

Freddie suddenly bolted toward the draperies near Fallon. "There's a door back of these. Leads to a basement and tunnel that goes out the back. I remember now."

Kenderson helped Fallon to spread the drapery area Freddie had pointed out. An outline of a door built flush into the rear wall could hardly be detected. A round, flush-mounted lock was the only indication it was an opening. Fallon quickly jimmied the lock with his crowbar and ripped the door open. Kenderson illuminated a light switch on the wall at the top of concrete stairs. He flipped it, and all three could see the steep stairs leading downward. A frightened woman's voice, called weakly, "Help me."

Fallon shouted, "That sounds like Sarah." A strange storage-like structure was mounted halfway down and to the side of the steps. The voice appeared to be coming from there. A slimmer padlock holding a hinged panel took only moments to cut off.

Avoiding shining the light in her face, Kenderson saw by the ceiling light Sarah MacCormick lying stricken on a bare wooden floor. A quick glance told him she had been badly beaten. Somehow, she found the strength to raise her head.

Get help. That rear door in the basement opens on a tunnel that leads outside. You can reach First Street through one of the backyards. That's how Setich brought me here. Hurry, for God's sake, hurry!" She sounded hysterical.

No way I'm going to leave you," Fallon assured her. "I can carry you out the tunnel."

She fell back on the floor. It took a moment for her eyes to focus on Fallon. "It's you? Oh, Al, it's so good....." Her words slurred.

Kenderson looked for Freddie. He was nowhere in sight. Hurrying back to the "bedroom", he glanced upward and saw a light at the top of a staircase. He mounted the inside stairs, calling the boy's name. As he reached the top, he saw Freddie kneeling in front of a large, open safe.

"There's nothing in the damn thing. Nothing."

Kenderson heard the familiar pressure in his voice, a sure sign Freddie was about to lose it. They had to get out and take Sarah MacCormick with them. Walking to the front window, he glanced to the street and felt his heart skip a beat as the headlights of a Mercedes sedan turned into Front Street. There was no way they were going to make it out the way they had come in.

Grabbing Freddie's arm, he moved down the stairs and through the basement door. "Fallon, a car's pulling into Front. We've got to get out of here. Do you want help carrying Sarah?"

He shook his head. Sarah was groaning with pain. When Fallon lifted her she cried out. "Leave me, save yourselves."

As Kenderson moved down the sheer steps, the underground coolness swept over his face. With Freddie in the lead, he had to stoop to avoid striking his head against the ceiling supports. Hurrying along the dark passage, the light from the basement grew dimmer. He aimed the beam rearward and saw Fallon struggling with Sarah. He guessed they had traveled about thirty feet when Freddie shouted. "I can see a little light above me, and, hey, a wood ladder, so we can climb out of this mother."

Lifting a simple wooden cover upon reaching the top of

the steps, Kenderson could see he had emcrgcd in the middle of the empty lot at the rear of the Front Street office. Hawkins had prepared for a fast getaway.

Fallon appeared below him. He held a nearly limp and moaning Sarah erect against the stairs. Kenderson, lying flat on his belly, was able to reach down and clasp his arms under hers and behind her back. With Fallon pushing and Kenderson pulling, they were able to draw her slowly through the opening. A moment later, she lay whimpering on the bare ground. Fallon pulled out his car keys and tossed them to Kenderson.

"Take Freddie and drive back along First. I'll carry Sarah between these two houses and meet you."

Grabbing an agitated Freddie by the arm, Kenderson urged him along as fast as he could. A dog barked as they trotted between the two rundown houses that once represented prime river front property. On First Street, Kenderson, tugging at Freddie, turned left heading for MacCormick. Freddie's resistance slowed the pace. By now, Setich or some of his henchmen must have entered the Front Street Office and were aware of what had happened. He turned to Freddie, almost shouting.

"Man, we've got to split out of here. We don't want to explain what happened to Arnie Setich, do we?"

His words must have gotten through because Freddie squirmed free and began to run. Kenderson, whose side was starting to ache from the exertion, turned right until he spotted Fallon's Ford near a street light. Once Kenderson unlocked the doors, Freddie jumped in and a moment later they headed west toward Front. As he turned left on First, Kenderson heard two quick shots. He slowed, peering through the darkness for Fallon and Sarah.

Pulling quickly to the curb between the two houses whose side yards he and Freddie had just run through, he waited, heart pounding. Did Fallon need his help? He got out of the car and approached the nearest house whose lights were on. A moment later, Fallon staggered out to the curb with Sarah in his arms. Kenderson swung the back door open and between them, placed Sarah gently on the back seat. Fallon climbed in beside her. "Let's go. I had to put a couple of shots into the tunnel to keep them down there."

Kenderson quickly U-turned and headed back to MacCormick, just as two men emerged between the houses. He instinctively crouched, expecting gun fire. He saw that Fallon was holding his police revolver and peering out the side window. Driving fast but slowing for the cross streets, he entered the Seven-Eleven parking lot and drove to the rear. Fallon slipped into the driver's seat. "I know a doctor who will help and keep quiet. You and the boy get the hell out of here."

The Ford sped out of the parking lot and Kenderson hustled Freddie into the passenger side of the Datsun and was soon heading toward Filloy. He wondered where the nearest drug store was located and decided Wal-Mart, six blocks further on Monroe, was the closest. Pulling to the curb in front of the big discount store, Kenderson hurried to the drug counter at the rear. "I need this refilled, please," he said, handing the bottle to the pharmacist. The older woman looked closely at the label and shook her head.

"I'm not sure about this."

Kenderson pulled out his gold badge case and opened the cover. "This is a prescription for an ADHD youngster who has used his last pill over four hours ago. He'll soon be out of control. Do you want me to bring him in the store?"

She shook her head and moved up short steps behind a glass partition. He could see her measuring pills into the prescription bottle. When she brought it back to the counter, Kenderson saw the bottle had only ten or twelve pills. Before he could protest, she said, "The prescription has run out. I've given you enough until a doctor can write you a new one."

He was about to protest, but getting Freddie out of sight was more important. "Can I get a paper cup for water?"

She silently handed him one from under the counter. "There's a fountain near the entrance."

Thanking her, he paused long enough to fill the cup half full before hurrying to the Datsun. Freddie was bouncing up and down on the seat, looking anxiously in the direction they'd just come.

Kenderson shook a pill out of the bottle and handed it to the boy. "Take it, quick. Here's water." Freddie tossed the pill in his mouth but his shaking was so severe he spilled half of the water before he managed a gulp.

Kenderson knew it would be several minutes for the medication to kick in. Freddie would be hungry soon but getting him to cover first was vital. Wal-Mart had a cafeteria and Kenderson decided to buy some sandwiches right here.

The waitress resented his pushing her to hurry but five minutes later he emerged with two tuna sandwiches and a large Coke.

"You'll be okay if I let you off on Filloy?"

Freddie's agitation was lessening and he nodded. Kenderson looked for a following car as he turned on Filloy. None was in sight. Driving to the end of the street he made a U-turn and slowed as he neared the bamboo grove.

"Phone me in the morning, okay? And keep taking your meds."

He didn't watch as Freddie slipped out of the passenger seat and ran toward the south side of the street. His first time alone in hours, he felt himself trembling. His exhaustion brought back memories of the endless hours in Nam, during the two months before his shattering wound ended his duty in the steaming, merciless jungles. He had lived through his fears by staying absorbed in his job. Today was the same, but now the delayed stress was getting to him. He suddenly found himself laughing. Some officer of the court! How many laws did I break today? But he had survived and so had Freddie. Were the video tapes real clues to solving Earl Hawkins' murder or another wild goose chase? Whatever, he needed to locate them soon. He knew the crisis was just beginning. Setich was no fool, he'd suspect Kenderson was involved in today's break in. What he wouldn't know was Sarah MacCormick's rescue was the work of Castro's detective, Al Fallon.

Fran was waiting in the garage as he got out of the Datsun. She looked pale as she gave him a quick kiss. "Somebody phoned. They wanted to know where you were. I asked for a name but the man hung up. What's happening?"

"Sarah is safe."

He felt a rush of joy, seeing the relief flood her pretty face. Quickly relating the events of the evening, Fran was shaking her head in disbelief before he finished.

"Was that what the phone call was about?"

"Maybe. I keep wondering if Phil Hawkins can stop this craziness."

"But every time you need his help, you can't reach him."

Kenderson nodded.

"The kids have already eaten and gone out with their friends. I said midnight was curfew."

Kenderson decided he needed a scotch and water. Sipping it calmed his jitters.

He'd almost finished the drink when the phone rang. Fran motioned for him to answer. He said hello and a smile grew on his face. "Let me take this in the office, okay?"

Covering the phone, he told Fran, "Speaking of the devil, this is Phil Hawkins. Hang up this phone when I answer and come to the office."

A moment later, Fran was leaning over the desk to better hear the conversation. Phil Hawkins was saying, "Arnie Setich phoned me a little while ago. He's really boiled about the break in at the Front Street office. He figures you and Freddie had some hand in it. He mentioned some guy named Fisher."

Kenderson was put off by Phil's matter-of-fact presentation. He heard his tone sharpen. "Sarah MacCormick was almost beaten to death. And are they still looking to kill Freddie?"

"It's a big mistake and I told them so. Arnie is so paranoid, he thinks Sarah overheard some plans about expanding the business and he was afraid she'd alert his competitors."

Kenderson glanced at Fran, shaking his head in disbelief. "And why does Freddie concern them? He doesn't know about any expansion plans."

"I'm sure he doesn't. But my guess is, they're afraid he might spill something during a cross examination on the witness stand." Kenderson replied.

It was Fran's turn to roll her eyes. Kenderson persisted. "When Freddie was going to the Meadows with Pete and Arnie, did he witness something they don't want broadcast? He's scared to death when the subject comes up. It's almost like he wants me to assure Arnie he'll never talk."

He heard Phil's easy laugh. "Crazy, isn't it? Look, I'll try to get Arnie to calm down and quit being suspicious of Sarah and Freddie. By the way, do you know where they are now?"

Kenderson felt a deep sense of relief when he answered. "I don't really know." He figured he'd better get everything off his chest, now that Phil had contacted him.

"Has Setich bought the Santa Inglesia police department? I reported Sarah MacCormick's kidnaping. When I checked later, there was no record I'd called 911. And why was Freddie's escape from the courtroom suppressed in the media? Was this the way your father did business?"

Kenderson was surprised at the sudden vigor in Phil's voice. "Dad never had to do stuff like that. He took care of things in a different way." Kenderson heard pride as the son spoke of his father. A moment later, Phil sounded depressed. "He's gone now. Nothing will ever be the same."

Kenderson said, "I'm sorry for your loss, but you and I know Freddie didn't do it. Have you any idea where some video tapes might be hidden? Freddie thinks they may hold a clue to who really murdered your father."

Phil's tone was sharp,"Videos, what videos? I never heard of any such thing. Is Freddie joking? I'm sure there were no such things left by my father."

Kenderson realized he'd touched a nerve. But why? Did Phil know about the blackmail videos? He sounded agitated. Better forget the tape issue and talk about stopping Setich.

"Can you get Arnie to let up on Freddie and Sarah? I don't see how they can be a threat to him."

Phil's, "I'll talk to him," sounded like he was down again.

"I've tried to phone you a number of times for help. Most of the time your answering machine isn't even on."

Phil's spirits seemed normal again, as he laughed. "Oh, that. I'm having a new system installed. It's the usual snafues. Should be okay now." After a brief pause, "Keep me posted on what's happening. And I'll insist Arnie call off his dogs, okay?"

Kenderson thanked Phil for phoning, promising to stay in touch. After he'd cradled the phone, Fran sat down in one of the side chairs Kenderson used for his clients. "What did you make of that?"

"I'd like to think he can control Setich. Life would get back to normal, and Freddie and Sarah could come out of hiding."

Fran wrinkled her nose."Would you let your phone system be down for days if you were running for office? And his moods. My Lord, they roller coastered from depressed to manic during a five minute phone call. He's a strange guy."

"He's suffered a big loss. Everyone says he worshiped his father." He looked at Fran's doubting expression."Of course, I'm not going to tell Phil about Fallon or anything else."

Fran nodded. "Good. Which leaves us where?"

"Back to who killed Earl Hawkins. Setich and Pete have airtight alibis. If they'd hired someone to kill Earl, he wouldn't let a stranger slug him from behind. It had to be someone he knew and trusted. The only leads left are those videos. If we uncover the names of his blackmail victims, we may have the killer." He watched Fran for her approval. After seeing a reluctant nod, he went on.

"I need to know what Sarah MacCormick overheard about the organization expanding. And what did Freddie witness? It had to be something Setich is deathly afraid will be exposed."

Fran said, "Can we drop all this for now?" She took his hand. "Honey, you look like what the proverbial cat dragged in." She gave a sexy leer. "And I have just the remedy. The kids won't be home for a couple of hours, so how about some of Fran's extra-special physical therapy and then later we order a big pizza?"

Kenderson grinned, "You've got a customer."

They were both laughing as Fran took his hand and led him toward the bedroom.

Later in bed, Fran gently touched his temple. "Lucky you, you've got all that gorgeous auburn hair. Your blue eyes are nice, too." He smiled, countering, "Nice everything. Great therapist, too."

Later, feeling relaxed for the first time in days, he wondered if Phil Hawkins would keep his word. Until he was sure, Freddie had to stay out of sight. His last thought, just before dropping into a deep sleep, was about the missing videos.

THURSDAY MORNING

Fran's Big Ben windup alarm clock went off at 6:30 and Kenderson, half asleep, fumbled for the phone on his night stand. Fran laughed."It's my clock, sleepyhead. You can enjoy fifteen minutes more and then I'll be back."

Now fully awake, his mind began to race. So much to do. Where should he start? Deciding that a shower and shave had priority, he stepped under a spray of warm water and lathered his thick head of hair. Later, shaving, he decided that he had to tell Washington what was happening. Nehi's approach was strictly logical, while his own approach to problems tended to be colored by emotions. He sternly told himself he must not mention the gray area of the law he found himself operating in yesterday.

Kenderson's hurried breakfast consisted of toast and coffee. He said goodby to his chattering teenagers before Fran walked him to the garage door. She looked tense. "I'm scared. Is Setich going to listen to Phil Hawkins? Will he come after us because you and Fallon snatched Sarah from his basement prison?"

Kenderson felt sick imagining Fran or the kids being hurt on his account. He tried to sound confident."I think Sarah is safe now. Finding who killed Earl is Freddie's only real salvation and ours."

He hugged her. He knew he sounded silly asking Fran to tell the kids to be careful. At their age, they felt invincible. She nodded, and her goodbye kiss was longer than usual.

At work, he looked at his calendar. Tonight the parents of his wards would meet in the conference room. He looked forward to these sessions because these single parents, grandparents and couples helped one another with new ideas, and just as important, emotional support.

He made several phone calls to parents who wanted to know how to deal with runaways. There were no easy answers. To call the cops was important, as was finding satisfactions in their own lives. That course of action sometimes turned out to be the best solution because it helped the parent emotionally disengage from the teenager. Surprisingly, when this happened, the teen and parent often began to interact on a more adult level.

Later in the morning he phoned an MD who contracted with the Diversion Center and asked for a new Ritalin prescription. After a few questions, the doctor said he would phone in the order to the Longs Kenderson had requested.

Farber walked in immediately after he'd hung up the phone. Incredibly, he was fairly affable and asked how Freddie had fared in court the day before. Kenderson had no good answer so he said the case had been continued. He could see Farber frown and start to ask why, when Marilyn called his name, saying he had a phone call.

As Farber walked away, Washington entered the front door. Kenderson waved him to his office. "Shut the door, okay? I want to bring you up to date."

He started cautiously, not wishing to tell Washington about Sarah MacCormick or how many risks he'd taken or laws he'd broken. He told him about Freddie's escape from the courtroom, which was never reported in the media.

"Why am I not surprised," Washington said. "Has this to do with Phil Hawkins' election campaign? Does he want Freddie to disappear until after November?"

"Maybe that. But Arnie Setich wants him gone, maybe permanently. Something to do with an event or crime Freddie may have witnessed when he was with Setich and Pete Hawkins at the Meadows. It sounds like they're afraid if he's ever put on the witness stand he'll talk about what happened. That puzzles me. Why would the boy want to talk about an old crime." He paused, thinking. "Unless it involved somebody very important."

"Or close to him?"

"Like, somebody he really liked? Who would that be? In reading his case history, there's nobody he ever seemed to love or trust.

"You mean after his mother died, or was killed as her sister keeps insisting."

"Are you thinking what I am?"

Washington nodded. "Did he recently begin to understand what was happening at the time? And now he's connecting events?"

"He must have said or done something recently that worries Setich."

"Why didn't Setich kill him before? He must have wanted to."

"Because Earl Hawkins wanted the boy alive?"

"Freddie's fair game, now his protection is gone."

"Do you know where he is?"

"Not really."

"How is your sleuthing going?"

"There's talk about video tapes Hawkins was using to blackmail important people in this community. One of them may have killed Hawkins or hired someone to do the job. If I could view them, we might have some answers."

"Back to basics. Has Freddie told you where he and Ermon were during those hours?"

Kenderson shook his head. "I haven't seen him long enough to ask. But I will."

Washington laughed. "I'll believe it when it happens."

He stood up and started out the door. "Keep me posted. And if I can help, I will."

Kenderson thought, you may regret that offer. There was no way of predicting who he'd have to ask for assistance. Kenderson made three more phone calls and was making notes for the night's meeting when the phone rang. Freddie sounded on a high. "I think I know where the old man hid his tapes. He was a slippery dude and this is just the kind of bullshit trick he'd pull."

"Man, slow down," Kenderson said gently. "Where are you? I need to deliver your Ritalin."

The pause was so long, Kenderson thought the boy had hung up on him. "Can you open a safe? An old one? Do you know somebody who can?"

"What safe, where?"

In the silence that followed, Kenderson guessed Freddie was weighing how far he could trust his social worker. Freddie's next words told him he was making progress. "Drive down to Eighth and park a block away from the Presbyterian Church. Walk until you see the wooden annex next to it. I'll watch for you. If you don't see me, keep going, okay?"

The dial tone told him the conversation was over. His heart started to pound. The videos. Was Freddie onto something? Had he been hiding in the annex building all this time? It made sense, because it was only a short walk from the bamboo patch on Filloy. An inner voice warned against sinking even further into the shadowy realm of criminal behavior. If Freddie had been hiding in the annex, he was obviously trespassing and god knows what else.

As he walked out the door, he told Marilyn he had an urgent home visit. "I'll phone in for messages."

His first stop was Long's Drug Store where he picked up the prescription of the small white pills that could keep Freddie on an even keel.

Kenderson drove past the white, steepled church twice and then circled the block one more time before parking on the corner of Fredrick and Eighth. He got out carrying his report book, pretending to look at addresses while consulting the small black binder. As he neared the annex, he saw a slight motion among the thick branches of the tall willow tree near the side the church. Freddie gave a brief wave and after glancing both ways, raced across the blacktop up the short flight of stairs and disappeared into the annex building, shutting the door after him.

Trying to look casual, Kenderson mounted the steps and pushed against the door. Being slightly ajar, it opened easily. Freddie was coming out of his skin. It worried Kenderson.

"Have you taken your Ritalin? If not, here's a full bottle so why not take one and settle down."

He expected a big argument from the boy but surprisingly, Freddie walked into the kitchen, took a glass from a cabinet over the sink and tossed a pill in his mouth, washing it down with water from the faucet.

"Follow me," he ordered, placing the glass in the sink. Freddie quickly mounted the stairs to the loft, Kenderson following close behind. At the top, Freddie pointed dramatically toward the ancient, cobweb-covered safe. "I'm betting the old man put the tapes in there, and then had the cobwebs put on to make it look like it hasn't been used in a hundred years."

Kenderson's hopes plummeted. Freddie's explanation was weird. Even if he was right, how were they supposed to open it. Freddie ran to the safe and tore away a handful of cobwebs, holding it up before Kenderson eyes. Looking closely, he could see very little dust. Were there machines that could duplicate cobwebs? Brushing away the tangle, Kenderson tried to turn the wood covered handle. It refused to move in either direction. There was enough daylight to see behind the safe. Moving the hymnals, Kenderson squatted low enough to read the name, Upjohn's Reliable Safe Co. Freddie was moving around nervously. "What does it say?"

Kenderson told him, while he fingered the plate which seemed to be loose. As he wriggled it further, a slip of paper fell out on the floor. Freddie picked it up and began reading numbers. "Two, right, twelve, left and twenty-six right." Freddie whooped so loud Kenderson held up his hand to signal quiet.

The numbers on the dial were hard to read and it took five attempts before the safe opened. Freddie's guess had been right. The safe was clear of dust and two video tapes in their covers sat on the middle shelf. Freddie was going ballistic and Kenderson knew he had to calm the boy before they could work out their next steps.

Removing the tapes, Kenderson closed the heavy safe door and tried to rearrange the cobwebs in their former pattern. "Help me, Freddie. You see what I'm trying to do."

Responding, the boy removed the top hymnals and brushed them against the cobwebs still left on the safe. In five minutes, they'd roughly restored the original pattern. Only the person who'd devised the cobweb disguise would know the safe had been opened.

Quickly moving down the stairs, Kenderson peered through the glassed top of the door. Freddie stood behind him. "Are you going to look at the tapes now?"

About to reply, Kenderson abruptly moved away from the glassed door. "Stay down, Freddie. Simstead just drove by. He must have followed me."

Pointing to a phone on the loft floor, Kenderson asked, "Is that the phone you've been using?" Freddie nodded.

Hastily mounting the stairs, he picked up the phone and dialed his own number. After two rings, he heard Fran's voice. "Honey, Simstead followed me. I can't leave Freddie here and I can't bring him home. Will you phone Mary Washington and ask if we could meet there in about fifteen minutes." He was about to hang up when he thought of Al Fallon. "Phone Al Fallon. Use the beeper number by the phone. Ask him to meet us there. Tell him I have two video tapes I want him to look at."

"You found them?"

"Yes, and this may be the lead we've been looking for."

Saying I hope so, Fran hung up.

Faced with the problem of getting back to his Datsun without Simstead spotting him, Kenderson admitted it was impossible. But what if he resumed his search for a mythical address, while Freddie picked up the car. The thought of a nervous ADHD boy driving his venerable Datsun made him cringe, but there didn't appear to be any other solution.

Handing his car keys to the boy, Kenderson said, "I'll be where I've been letting you off on Filloy behind the bamboos. I'll leave here and start walking down Eighth as I was doing before. Simstead will start watching me. When he turns the block, I'll duck into the alley. Make a run for the car when he's out of sight. See you on Filloy, okay?"

Kenderson was relieved to see the Ritalin had calmed Freddie. He went over the instructions and had the boy repeat them. Returning to the window, he waited until Simstead drove past and then walked back to the street, moving north on Eighth. He pretended to be absorbed in looking for an address but was aware that the next time the Cadillac went by, it slowed. He was sure Setich's goon had spotted him. As the Cadillac turned the next corner, Kenderson hurried into the alley and hid behind a rusting dumpster.

Cautiously peering out from behind the flaking metal, he saw the Cadillac had speeded up. Simstead must be pissed to have lost his quarry. He fervently hoped Freddie had made it unseen to the Datsun and would be waiting on Filloy. Running as fast as his lamed knee would allow, he turned into the vacant lot and moved behind the shelter of the bamboos. Peering out, he saw his Datsun slowly advancing toward him. Glancing up and down Filloy, he made sure no cars were in sight before stepping into the street and flagging down Freddie. Hurrying to the drivers side, he slipped behind the wheel, making a quick U-turn and then a right on Second.

Driving on a thoroughfare like Monroe would be the faster way to the Washington's, but staying on Second with it's frequent stop signs would be slower but safer.

Following the street paralleling the Oso River proved to be difficult because of frequent dead ends requiring detours to Third and sometimes Fourth. They made slow progress south toward Washington's home which was located in a recently developed subdivision. Simstead, by now, must have guessed his quarry had escaped by driving the side streets. On the outskirts of town, Second to Fifth Streets were blocked by an underpass requiring him to drive east to Monroe. Once there, he was able to increase speed. Two miles further, he made a right turn on Pond Street, and in three more blocks, turned into the Sunrise subdivision with its curving streets and frequent cul-de-sacs. Washington's home was the last house on Fremont Circle but Kenderson parked several houses away. Carrying the two tapes under his arm and with Freddie following, they both raced to the front door of 7001 and rang the bell.

Mary Washington opened the door immediately and, looking anxious, shooed them inside. "What's this all about? Fran's phone call scared hell out of me." Turning to Freddie, she asked, "Is this young man we have heard so much about?"

Kenderson held his breath, waiting for a defiant reply from his ward but the boy's eyes were glued to the cassettes.

"Let's see whose balls the old man was bustin'."

"Let me call Fran and see if Fallon will be coming. He walked to the kitchen and dialed his home. Fran sounded breathless. He could hear the fear in her voice as she told him Fallon would be interested in viewing the cassettes. "So I think he wants you to wait."

He hung up and, at Mary's invitation, everyone moved to the front room and sat around a small coffee table. Freddie began bouncing on the couch and Kenderson checked to see if he was due another Ritalin pill. Freddie said in two hours. Kenderson decided there was little point in holding back. Despite not wanting to enmesh them in his troubles, he had, in fact, made Nehi and Mary accessories to whatever he did now or in the future.

Mary showed her nervousness. Kenderson guessed that, like Nehi, she still wondered if this squirmy boy had killed his adoptive father. Kenderson briefly told her about the 911 call which had been suppressed, but soft pedaled the damage done to Sarah MacCormick. He was direct in telling her that Freddie's life was in danger and he, Kenderson's, actions may have put his own family at risk. "We'll get out of here as soon as possible so you won't be in the same boat."

He made up his mind at that moment to insist Freddie explain his whereabouts at the time of Earl Hawkins' murder, as well as what he had witnessed at the Meadows when he went there with Pete and Arnie Setich.

The sound of a key turning in the lock froze everyone. The laughter of relief followed as Nehi's big frame filled the doorway. The smaller Al Fallon followed him into the living room.

"So, you've got the videos. Let's look at them," Nehi said, picking up the TV remote and sitting down, indicating Fallon join him. In an aside to Kenderson: "Our beloved boss is afraid you're going to ruin his image. Somebody phoned, according to Marilyn, and told him you're still working with Mr. Hawkins, here." His affectionate pat on Freddie's shoulder didn't stop the bouncing.

Washington introduced Al Fallon to his wife. "Al told me he'd already met Freddie." The remark brought a grin to the boy's face."

"We did some cool stuff, man, right?"

Fallon nodded. "Sarah is physically recovering, but it will take years before she'll get over the mental trauma."

When Mary looked curious, Nehi said, "Fill you in later."

Nehi rose and put the first tape in the VCR and punched the play button. As the tape rolled, faint music could be heard in the background. The murky scene on the TV appeared to be somewhere in a night club, with the camera focusing on two figures, an older man and a young woman wearing tight shorts and naked from the waist to her long blonde hair. From their garbled talk, Kenderson guessed they were under the influence of drugs or alcohol. Freddie had stopped bouncing and stared at the screen, which caused Kenderson to say, "Cool it, okay?" Freddie's bouncing started in again.

Just as Washington was saying, "Who's the guy?" The camera zoomed in closer framing the man's face. "I don't

Robert White

believe it. That's Ray Zacherman, head of the Zacherman Title Company. He's also the Chairman of the Republican County Central Committee."

The tape continued, with shots of the girl unzipping Zacherman's fly and fondling him. The camera did a close up and Freddie shouted gleefully "The guys got a little, tiny dick. Like he's never going to be able to bonk her."

"Thank you for that observation," Kenderson said, " And will you shut the hell up, okay?" Freddie became quiet but his bouncing continued.

The tape was more of the same until Washington punched the stop button. "Lets look at the other one." He hit rewind, and a moment later removed the first tape and inserted the second one.

The scene looked familiar and so did the girl. They were unable to make out the man until the camera zoomed for a closeup. Washington again sounded shocked. "That's Henry Phillips. He owns the biggest department store in town. And, would you believe, he's Chairman of the County Democratic Central Committee." Washington glanced around the room, shaking his head, "Hawkins had both sides in his pocket. No wonder his candidates never lost a local election."

The camera zoomed to the unlucky man's crotch. Kenderson put a preventive hand on Freddie's arm, hoping to forestall further comments.

The camera suddenly panned away from Henry Phillips, focusing on a shadowy figure in the background. A heavy set man with glazed eyes suddenly looked up, and drunkenly charged in the direction of the videographer. The camcorder must have been knocked to the floor because the final frames showed blurred chair legs.

Kenderson looked at Washington, "Do you recognize the last man?"

Washington shook his head and turned to Al Fallon. "Does the guy look familiar to you?" Fallon said, "No."

Washington rewound the tape and ran the final frames several more times. Kenderson moved closer to the TV. Could this burly guy have killed Hawkins as payback for trying to frame him? Who was he? How could he be identified?

He turned to Al Fallon. "Is the picture clear enough for you to get an ID?"

"Maybe it could be enhanced and printed. But if the guy had no record, we'd be spinning our wheels."

Mary suddenly spoke up, "Honey," she said to Nehi, "Run it again please, and stop when he gets closest to the camera."

Washington did as she asked, stopping on the frame showing the largest picture of the man's face.

Mary studied the blurry picture in silence for almost thirty seconds, and then slowly said, "It couldn't be."

Kenderson said,"Couldn't be who?" Do you recognize the guy?"

"It just couldn't be who I think it is."

"Hon, spare us the suspense," Nehi said, "Who the hell is it?"

"I swear it looks like Reverend Edward Nichols, pastor of the First Presbyterian Church. He's a big guy, a former football player. Why in the world would Earl Hawkins have wanted to frame Nichols?"

Nehi said. "He's one of the most popular, influential guys in the county. If Hawkins had him in his pocket....."

Kenderson was surprised when Freddie calmly said, "My Mom and I used to go there when I was a kid. It does look like him."

Kenderson felt his spirits plummet. Could either of these three pillars of the community be capable of murdering Earl

Hawkins? They would have been admitted to the Hawkins' library without arousing suspicion. Or would Hawkins have been on guard with them? According to everyone, he was arrogant and ruthless. He must have thought none of his victims would have the guts to defy him. He looked at Fallon. "So where do we go from here?"

"We could check their alibis," Fallon said. "We'd have to think up some logical explanation for wanting them to account for last Sunday afternoon."

"Can you do that?" Washington asked.

Fallon thought for a moment. "We could say we were looking for witnesses to a car accident in a different location. People will deny they were at a certain location but if we press a little, will tell us what they were doing at the time. "

"So you'd look for a guilty reaction or an evasive reply?" Kenderson asked.

"Something like that. Then we'd do some phoning, maybe need leg work to check out a questionable story."

Everyone seemed to agree this was probably the only way to check the alibis of the three men they'd viewed on video tape without causing panic.

Washington and Fallon left together. Freddie had gone to the bathroom. Standing at the door, Mary looked at Kenderson with something akin to admiration. "He's quite a handful. How do you do it?"

Kenderson grinned. "Don't ask. I don't know. I keep thinking about a new job."

His tone turned serious. "I'm so sorry to involve you in this. Thanks for coming to the rescue. And be careful. The guys who are after Freddie are pros."

"Where will you take him?"

"I'm not sure. Setich will know by now where he's been hiding. I can't go back there."

"Would they look for him here?"

"Not unless Simstead followed me. I didn't see his Cadillac on my tail. But Mary, this could be dangerous."

She shrugged. "Maybe it's time to change things in Santa Inglesia, so people don't have to live in constant fear of thugs like Setich and Pete Hawkins."

"Mary, can I leave him here for a day or two?"

She nodded.

"And Nehi, will he kill me for doing this?"

"Let me take care of that, okay?"

"I'm going to ask you to excuse us for a few minutes. I have to ask Freddie about the murder, and some other things he knows, that have put his life in danger. I don't want you to hear any of this in case you're questioned."

Mary nodded and left the room, closing the door behind her. Kenderson motioned to Freddie to sit down in a chair opposite. "Freddie, no more stalling. Where were you and Ermon when Earl Hawkins was killed?"

The boy put on a stubborn face and started his fuck you routine, when Kenderson moved in front, grabbed his shoulders, and shook him till his head wobbled. "I haven't time for this! Where were you?"

The shaking and angry tone surprised the boy. He looked at Kenderson with surprise. "Alright, already. You going to help me even if I tell you where me and Ermon were?"

"Of course. So tell me."

Freddie lowered his head, his voice was barely audible. "We were in the house."

"When he was killed?"

"I guess so. We didn't hear nothing. I didn't know he was dead until you picked me up."

"Did you see or hear anyone?"

"We were playing some rap and stuff real loud."

Robert White

"Was the library door open or closed?"

"Shit, I don't know."

"Did Earl let you play music loud like that?"

"He always kept the library door closed. It's soundproof."

Kenderson nodded. He'd heard the police say that on Sunday night. "So you and Ermon drove down to the Meadows about four thirty?"

Freddie nodded. "About then, maybe a little later."

So the murder took place about four, Kenderson thought. He'd tell Fallon what he'd found out.

Facing Freddie, Kenderson said, "Why does Setich want to kill you?" To Kenderson's surprise, he saw tears starting. Freddie choked when he started to talk. "He knows I figured out he helped kill my Mom."

It was Kenderson's turn to be stunned. "Can you tell me about it?"

Haltingly, Freddie told his story. "The night my Mom died, I went with Arnie and Pete to the Meadows to collect money from the store owners. In a junky looking drug store we went to last, the owner told Arnie he had a phone call. He took it in the back so I didn't hear what was said. When he came back, he took Pete aside and said something to him. I didn't hear that either."

The tears were starting again. Freddie struggled to finish. "When they came back, Arnie said the old man wanted a drug prescription filled for my mom because she wasn't sleeping good. I remember he said it funny, like he was thinking something weird." The boy was fighting heavy tears. Kenderson waited and then encouraged him to go on.

"Arnie took the guy behind the drug counter and told him to do something. I heard the guy say "no" and then Arnie hit him hard. The guy hollered like he was dying, but went to the back room and pretty soon came back carrying a little bottle with pills in it. Arnie told me it would help mom sleep better."

Freddie began sobbing. "Those pills killed her."

"How do you know that?"

"I found them in her pillow case the morning she died. She must have stuffed them there when she realized she'd been drugged."

"Her pillow case?" Freddie nodded.

"They fought a lot before she died. They had separate bedrooms. The old man thought she was cheating and was always snooping around for letters or notes to prove it."

Kenderson thought Freddie had lost it. What had one to do with the other? "What are you saying?"

"My mom used to write me notes about being good, and things she, like, hoped we could do together. She'd put them in my pillow case when no one was around. When I wanted to let her know some secret, I'd do the same."

"So why do you say the pills killed her?"

"I didn't figure that out until a little while ago. I thought she'd O.D.'d on her regular sleeping pills. Mrs. Nabors told the medics the bottle had been full the night before and in the morning they found it empty on the floor."

"So what did you recently figure out?"

"The pills I found looked like her regular ones, but when I went to the pharmacy and asked the guy who Arnie got the pills from that night, he had a shit fit. Swore he knew nothing about no pills. I told him I was there and saw it. When I said I'd tell Arnie he'd snitched, he admitted there was lots more codeine in those pills than the ones you buy over the counter. He said he'd pay me not to let Arnie know he'd talked."

"What happened to the druggist?"

"Last time me and Ermon went in there, they told me he'd left town." Freddie fought angry tears.

"I went crazy after mom died. That's when I really started to fuck up. Having the doctor tell me I was hyper made it easier. I'm sure my old man wanted mom dead because one night, I heard her threaten to call Sacramento about how he'd fleeced the MacCormicks and then killed her father."

"You heard the fight?" Freddie nodded.

"The old man went nuts. Told her he'd kill her if she went to the state lawyer's office in Sacramento."

"You mean the Attorney General's Office?"

"Yeah, I guess that's what it's called."

"So what made Arnie suspect you'd discovered he'd switched the sleeping pills?"

"The old man never changed mom's room. Told people it was a shrine. One day I found a couple of sleeping pills on the floor behind the toilet when I was looking for something in her medicine cabinet." The boy paused, his face etched with hatred. "Arnie saw me coming out of her bedroom. He made me show him the pills in my hand. He joked, asking if I was doing Mrs. Nabors' job now. I laughed, but he must have seen something different in my eyes."

"Whoever switched the sleeping pills must have worried about what happened to the lethal pill container?"

"It didn't matter after the medical examiner and coroner decided it was suicide. Besides, Pete was always fucking up on jobs. Arnie and the old man must have figured he'd lost the bottle somewhere."

"And right after Arnie saw you with the pills, Earl Hawkins was killed?" Freddie nodded.

"One more thing, did your mom trust Phil?"

"I guess so, but he was never around."

Kenderson had run out of queries for the moment. Within minutes, his most troublesome and exasperating ward had cleared up a host of questions. The boy seemed almost calm, when Kenderson expected him to be on the ceiling. My Lord, Kenderson wondered, is Freddie Hawkins beginning to trust me?

Another question dawned on him. "What about the autopsy? Surely, the medical examiner would know what kind of pills had killed your mom?"

Freddie shrugged his shoulders. "He's probably on the organization payroll. The report said it was suicide. End of questions."

Kenderson put his hand Freddie's shoulder. "Thanks for talking to me." The boy instinctively shrugged off the gesture of affection. Then, as if apologizing, he said, "I been wanting to tell somebody, but I didn't know who to trust."

Kenderson walked to the kitchen door and knocked. Mary opened it and came into the front room. Looking at their faces she said, "A good session?"

Kenderson said it was. "I've got to leave now. Will you be all right?" A firm nod of her head told him she was prepared to help him to the end.

Turning to Freddie, he said, "You'll be fine. Don't go out, and don't phone Ermon and let him know where you are. If he's questioned, he'll tell."

Freddie said, "Okay." Kenderson, on impulse, wanted to shake his hand as an equal partner. Deciding the boy needed time to deal with his new, fragile feelings, he didn't.

THURSDAY AFTERNOON

Back in the Datsun, he cautiously drove away from the Washington's, through a series of side streets, avoiding boulevards that connected to the southern section of the city. If Simstead spotted him, he wanted it to be in the opposite part of Santa Inglesia.

Nearing the Diversion Center, he realized it was after twelve and entered the drive-thru section of a Burger King near the Diversion Center. He ordered the Whopper and french fries, deciding to hell with cholesterol. He parked a short way down the street and finished his meal, then continued on, ending in the parking lot of the Center.

As he was getting out of his car, he spotted Simstead's Cadillac entering behind him. For a moment, he thought of getting back in the Datsun and trying to shake the man. He decided that would be senseless because the goon knew where he worked.

Simstead parked next to him and, as he slowly got out of his car, Kenderson realized he would be no match physically for this young, well muscled guy. The big man got to the point. "So where's the kid? Thought you were pretty smart, taking the side streets."

Kenderson felt relief that he hadn't been spotted near Washington's. "What do you want? You're not related to him and neither is your boss. If I deal with anyone in the family, it will be Phil."

"He ain't your business anymore. Your boss told me that."

Thank you, Farber, he thought, for your ever helpful assistance. "So what do you want?"

"Just tell me where you stashed him."

"And if I don't?"

You got two kids. And I know you don't want nothin' happening to them or that pretty wife of yours.

He felt a moment of sickening fear, replaced by a blind rage he hadn't experienced since he was a boy confronting his army colonel father. Sudden, surprising words came out of his mouth. "Don't touch them or I'll kill you."

Simstead, surprised, took a step backward. He quickly recovered. "A tough guy. Tell me where the kid is. We just want to talk to him. He won't be hurt."

"I don't believe you. I'm going in and phone Phil. If he will be there when you talk to the boy, I'll discuss a possible meeting with Freddie. Until Phil and the boy agree it's safe to meet with Arnie, my ward will stay out of sight."

Simstead's face flushed as he cut off a reply. Retreating to the sedan, he sped out of the parking lot.

Kenderson found himself trembling from the release of pent up anger. My God, he thought, how many times did I want to say those words to my old man. He quickly walked up the flagstone steps into the Center said a quick "Hi" to Marilyn, and entered his office, shutting the door. It was not a good time to meet Farber. He told himself, this craziness has got to stop and Phil is the only one who can make it happen.

He dialed, fearing he was about to hear prolonged ringing. After the sixth one, Phil Hawkins answered.

"It's Kenderson, Phil. Simstead has been playing tag with me all day, trying to get his hands on Freddie. I thought you were going to talk to Arnie and get him to cool it."

Phil sounded earnest. "I can't get hold of the man. Believe me, I've been trying. If something tragic happens, the negative publicity could force me out of the race."

"Phil, something tragic did happen to Sarah MacCormick. She's lucky to be alive. And why are they so anxious to get their hands on Freddie? He's not going to spill any beans." Even as he said it, Kenderson realized he could not guarantee what Freddie would do. The boy's deep rage against his mother's killers made his actions unpredictable. What was worse, if the DA's office found out, they would have a solid motive for proving his client was the killer.

Phil said, "Arnie thinks he can run everything himself now, but he's wrong. I've pointed out to him that if elected, I'll have lots of influence which he and Pete can share. I'm hoping he'll listen. Selfishly, I don't want any notoriety connected to the Hawkins name." There was a long silence before Phil, sounding wistful, said, "Things happened in the past I didn't know about and wouldn't have approved. I was in law school and later up in Sacramento and busy with a lot of pro bono work." His voice sounded sad, as it trailed off. Kenderson sensed the man wanted to say more but Phil ended the conversation abruptly, "I'll be in touch."

Strange, Kenderson thought, wondering if Phil was unaware of how others might react to his odd behavior. Hardly good qualities in an aspiring politician. What a strange family. Earl Hawkins had raised a model citizen in Phil, and from all accounts, a nobody in his other son, Pete, who moved in Arnie Setich's shadow. And what was the real relationship between Phil and Arnie? Phil said he disapproved of Setich and didn't like the fact that his father had made him a close partner in the business. Businesses, apparently. One was on the surface, the other a shadowy organization extorting money from ghetto merchants. Phil's last words suggested he was not in control, and to have any influence, he was forced to make deals with Setich on a quid pro quo basis. The more he thought about it, the more it shook him. The truth hit him violently. Phil Hawkins lacked the power to protect anyone. Not Freddie, or me, or my family. That left Castro and Fallon, and if the powers in the police department discovered they were secretly helping, it would be all over for everybody.

Kenderson rocked his swivel chair back, hoisted his brown, size elevens onto the green, metal desk and told himself to relax. It didn't work, because his mind wouldn't let go of the nightmare of the past four and a half days. He reflected dubiously, the only good thing to happen was winning a tiny measure of confidence from the most difficult boy on his caseload. Or, he guessed, anyone's caseload.

He wondered if Fallon had been able to check the alibis of the three prominent citizens they'd viewed on tape that morning. Probably too early. He thought of Sarah, who liked attending his weekly parent sessions, and felt a chill run up his spine. The brutal beating by Setich and his men sent a frightening warning to everyone involved in the case. He suddenly thought of asking Farber for permission to carry a gun. A recent law authorized Probation Officers to carry concealed weapons when their duties took them into daily contact with violent probationers. He dismissed the idea at once. First of all, his wards were not considered violent, just the opposite, and Farber would laugh at his request. He regretted that he could not level with the man about the danger he and Freddie were really in.

The phone rang and to his surprise, Fallon was on the other end. He spoke quietly, as though fearful of being overheard."The two politicians' alibis checked out. I told them we had the tapes and planned no further action. They were nervous as hell about other copies existing, and I told them my guess was there weren't any. I warned them to talk to no one about their video taped fling in LA and assured them we knew they had been set up for blackmail by the late Earl Hawkins."

"So what about Edward Nichols?"

"The guy was short with me, seemed annoyed as hell I'd bothered him. He refused to give information regarding his whereabouts last Sunday afternoon. I'm checking some old rap sheets. His name rings a bell." Suddenly, Fallon's voice got louder. "Yes, Sergeant, I'll check that out." The buzz of the dial tone told Kenderson someone had come within earshot, triggering the faked conversation and the quick hang up.

Fran should be home and, wanting to be sure she and the kids were all right, he called and getting no response after a number of rings, was about to hang up when he heard Fran's breathless voice. "I can't find Bandit! I've been trotting up and down the block. I don't know what got into her. She's too old and lazy go out in the front yard. The kids are with their friends and I'm sure they didn't take her along."

"Do you think she crawled off somewhere to die?"

"I'll look around but I doubt that's what happened." The silence was strained. "You don't suppose Setich's goons would kill her as a warning to us."

Kenderson's spirits plunged. He felt helpless. A boy again, facing an overpowering father. The next moment, his anger took over. "Keep looking and let me know when you find her."

Fran sounded discouraged and angry. "For God's sake, can't somebody find out who killed Earl Hawkins! We can't keep living like this!"

After telling Fran he was sorry for creating this situation, there was nothing more to say. He cradled the phone, feeling like a failure. Who killed Earl Hawkins? Now there was another suspect in Reverend Edward Nichols, pastor of the First Presbyterian Church of Santa Inglesia. And, before his hasty hang up, Fallon had said his name rang a bell. Could the good reverend have a past criminal record which would somehow pinpoint his being the killer? That would have to wait until Fallon had checked old rap sheets. Was the crime motivated by the so-called expansion project the Hawkins' organization was planning? The more he thought about it, the project seemed to concern everybody. Even Phil, who admitted he was never included in the inner circle, seemed distressed by whatever was in the works.

He thought about the missing cat and was in the process of speculating about what it all meant, when Washington walked through the door. Relieved to have someone he could trust to talk to, he lowered his feet and rose out of his chair, happy to get away from the Diversion Center and his troubling thoughts. "I've eaten, but I'll go with you and have a coke," he said, starting toward the entrance. "I'll even drive."

"Do you think your automobile can make it four blocks?" Washington jibed. "When are you going to give up on that wreck and buy something reliable."

"Reliable? That Datsun's done way over two hundred thousand miles. That's reliable." They waved to Marilyn, who was grinning at the familiar banter.

Once in the car, Washington's manner changed. "Jay, I'm worried as hell having Freddie in my house. Mary is a natural born rescuer and she wants to help. But I don't think she realizes how dangerous harboring this desperate kid can be."

"I agree, and I'm debating on how to get him moved without Setich and his thugs finding out. I want to do it legally but I don't know if Judge Smithers is on Setich's payroll. Even if he isn't, he may insist on Farber okaying his being moved to another location."

Kenderson drove into a parking space adjacent to the Burger King and shut off the engine. "Gertrude Manners is the other juvenile judge. She's pretty lenient but she's also pretty naive. If I tell her the whole story, she'll get excited and make a bunch of phone calls to find out if I'm telling the truth. She won't know what she's talking about, and all she'll get will be denials."

Washington nodded his head. "I'm sure you're right. So what else can happen?"

"Sarah MacCormick may have a friend or relative away from Santa Inglesia where he'd temporarily be safe. Her family's been in this area for generations."

"Good thinking. But can you reach her and will she be able to talk."

"I'll get in touch with Fallon and have him ask her."

Washington nodded and Kenderson got out of the car, returning a few minutes later with a Whopper and two cokes.

Back at the Diversion Center, the two split up, each entering his own office. Kenderson closed his door and dialed Fallon's number. The latter's voice dropped to a near whisper, the moment he recognized who was calling. Kenderson quickly conveyed his message and was reassured the lady would be questioned.

He felt a moment of relief and then, eyeing the stack of phone messages on his desk, began returning the calls. A number of them were from anxious parents wanting quick answers to questions that would take more than advice to settle. He promised each of them that time would be reserved that evening for problems that could be resolved through group discussion.

When he realized he had spent well over an hour on phone calls, he decided he'd better catch up on his progress reports. He was halfway through this task when line three on his phone began to blink. He had given this special number to several of his parents who hated having their phone calls go through a receptionist. He had also given it to Sarah MacCormick. He felt nervous as he reached for the phone. It was Sarah, sounding rested, like she was starting to recover from the brutal beating. "Officer Fallon said you wanted me to call."

"Thank you for getting in touch. You sound better and I hope you're recovering." She thanked him for his concern and he continued.

"Freddie isn't safe in Santa Inglesia. I wondered if you have out-of-town relatives who might take him until things are more secure here."

There was a silence before she said," My cousin, Arlene MacCormick, married a Robert Converse who is a successful farmer near Bakersfield."

"Would she be willing to take him temporarily?"

"I think so. I'll phone her and ask." She hesitated before saying, "My father's brother, Miller MacCormick, left town with his family soon after Earl Hawkins came to Santa Inglesia. He was outraged when my father sponsored Hawkins in the community and encouraged his courting Clarissa. There's never been any visiting between the brothers or their families after that. Arlene and I were close childhood friends and I've written to her over the years, but my Uncle Miller would never lift a finger to help us after we were swindled and my father murdered. Arlene told me her father had said my father had gotten just what he had asked for."

"Your cousin, Arlene, doesn't agree with her father?"

Robert White

"No, she doesn't, and my uncle is old now and unable to run everyone's life like he used to." She paused, "I miss coming to the group meetings. Maybe I can get there before it's over and give you directions to Arlene's home."

Kenderson felt his throat tighten and he started to warn her against being seen in public, but she had already hung up. He wanted to call her back but he realized he didn't know how to reach her. Frustrated, he dialed Fallon's number but the officer on the desk said he was gone for the rest of the day and couldn't be reached.

It was nearly four o'clock. He thought about going home and coming back for the six-thirty parent meeting. First, he'd talk to Washington.

He knocked before walking into his friend's office. Nehi was absorbed in scoring a Rorschach test and looked impatient at being interrupted. Kenderson shut the door and moved closer to the desk.

"Sorry, but I was sure you'd want to know, I may have found a safe place for Freddie out of town."

Nehi signaled for him to sit down. "Sorry to be testy, but this kid sees no butterflies or elephants or anything usual in the ink blots. He creates images out of tiny, peripheral areas that are almost invisible. His responses will wow my psych prof no end."

Washington stood up and stretched. "That's good news, and thanks for getting it done in a hurry. Mary tells me the boy is a handful before he takes his Ritalin."

Kenderson thought about telling his friend that Bandit was missing, but didn't, hoping that the venerable animal had merely decided to take an unaccustomed jaunt into the front yard. Kenderson stood up.

"Going home. Be back at six thirty. Will you be here?"

"Probably not. Thanks again."

Kenderson was thankful he wasn't asked where he intended to hide Freddie. Driving home, he watched his rearview and side mirrors. In the past few days it had become an automatic reflex. He thought about Sarah risking a meeting with him after the evening's session. Was she becoming careless? He wondered if the Reverend Nichols was a likely suspect. Fallon would have an informed opinion about that. He parked in the driveway and looked up and down the street for the errant cat, hoping she had returned on her own.

Fran looked alarmed when he walked in the front door. "You're home early, is something wrong?" He hugged her and she clung to him, trembling.

"No, not really. I think I can get Freddie out of town soon. Maybe that will cool things off. And Bandit, did she come home?"

"No, I've phoned one or two neighbors and when the kids come home, I'll ask them to knock on doors to see if Bandit took refuge in someone's yard." Fran looked tearful. "That cat drives me crazy with her insistent demands for food, but I'd miss her something awful if she wasn't here."

Kenderson agreed. Even though you were in the act of emptying a can of cat food in her dish, she kept up her persistent meowing. Strange. And lateness in feeding her earned you proportionately higher decibels.

Robert White

THURSDAY EVENING

Kenderson decided not to share any details with Fran about Sarah MacCormick's help or where Freddie would be going. Fran said she'd fix a quick dinner, this being a meeting night, and while waiting he walked back to the den, sat down, pulling out his list of suspects. He added the name of Edward Nichols and started to cross Freddie's name off, then hesitated, deciding not to come to any conclusions until he knew more. The boy *had* been in the house when Hawkins was murdered.

He had just finished a bowl of chili and crackers when the kids came home. Their faces grew serious as Fran told them about Bandit being gone. Cindy was near tears. "Mom, somebody must have taken her. She's so old, all she wants to do is sleep in her box. There isn't anything that would make her go out to the front yard and wander away."

Kenderson felt a chill of fear. Cindy was right. Fran's and the kid's faces told him they were equally apprehensive. Shit! When was this craziness going to end? Hopefully, when neither Sarah or Freddie were seen as threats to the organization.

On his way out the door, he tried to think of something of comforting to say to his family, but the words would have been empty. He embraced Fran and briefly put his arms around the shoulders of Vernon and Cindy, saying he hoped this would all be over soon. As he drove off, all three were standing in the doorway watching. He fought his tendency to repeat his,"I'm no good, because I let people down" litany. What I need is to get real pissed off, he told himself. And act quick and, God help us all, smart.

Ten of the fifteen parents were on hand by six thirty. Only two or three couples usually attended, because the majority of fathers thought group discussions were a waste of time. "Give 'em a good kick in the ass when they screw up," was a familiar phrase. The men who did attend found themselves sharing frustrations with the single fathers in the group, and as time went on, be pleased to learn how effective a unified parent approach worked. Kenderson enjoyed working with the parents because the majority were demoralized by their offsprings' school failures and senseless defiance. Often, drug and alcohol abuse made everything worse. The parents provided emotional support to one another, which meant willingness to try different approaches. Most of all, he enjoyed their bonding with him and one another. Invariably, the parent who came for the first time left with heartfelt relief saying, "Thank God, I'm not the only failure as a parent."

The group was coming to a close, with characteristic laughter as one single mother told of a small triumph in getting her son to class that week. Facing the door of the conference room, which had been left open because of the heat, Kenderson was startled to see Sarah MacCormick scurry by, heading for his office. His expression caused the mother who had been talking to stop. "Did I say something wrong?"

"No, not at all. It was something unrelated to what you were saying. Congratulations, on getting Jim to school."

The parents left shortly afterward, but he could hear comments being exchanged in the parking lot, which was usual. Some parents arranged to meet for coffee and more talk.

Sarah still wore her bruises but they were lighter in color. He started to admonish her for taking the risk of showing up in person, but anticipating this, she said. "Al is close by. I had to talk him into coming, but I wanted to be sure to give you written directions to follow. So take this paper. It will explain exactly how to get to my cousin's farm, which is about ten miles from Bakersfield along county roads." She hesitated, as though wanting to say more. Kenderson realized this might be his only chance to find out what else she knew about what the organization was planning.

"Sarah, as long as you're here, was there anything else you overheard that might help me find Hawkins' killer? What was supposed to happen? And who did it involve? Was Phil to be part of it?"

Sarah sighed. "As I told you, I only heard snatches of talk. Phil wasn't at the meeting I'm talking about, but I think he was supposed to do something. Earl suggested whatever it was, and Arnie and Pete went along. That's all I really know. Sorry I couldn't be more help."

"Be careful when you leave," Kenderson warned her. He got to his feet, but Sarah remained seated. "Al wants you to give me a ride to Fremont Street. He'll meet us there. He wants to talk to you about the best way to get Freddie out of Santa Inglesia without being followed. He said tonight might be the best time to go."

Kenderson started to object but decided to hear what Fallon had to say. He put the directions in his pocket and after surveying the street outside the Center for suspicious cars, Kenderson took Sarah's arm and hurried to the Datsun. Lower Fremont was a hangout for winos and homeless men, located on the edge of the Meadows. Kenderson pulled up behind Fallon's unmarked police car and helped Sarah out the passenger door, after which she walked to the police car and got in. Fallon approached. "Did Sarah tell you tonight may be our best bet for getting the kid out of town?"

Kenderson nodded. "Why tonight?"

"My guess is Setich won't be looking for anything to happen this fast." Kenderson nodded.

"I'll phone my wife on the cellular and let her know I won't be home."

Fallon was abrupt. "I'll let her know. Don't use your cellular at all. They've probably been monitoring your signal for days."

Kenderson's stomach tightened. He wanted to tell Fallon about Bandit's being gone, but the officer had taken over.

"We've got to assume Simstead will be on your tail, once you pick up Freddie. They've got too many informants on the payroll, in and out of the Meadows. One of them is bound to spot you. They'll know the make of your car and what you look likc and what the kid looks like. So we'll have to do some different stuff ourselvcs."

"Like what?"

"Like heading north in one hell of a hurry. Not south, which is where you'll be going eventually." Kenderson started to interrupt, but Fallon held up his hand. "Save the questions. We'll let him follow you out of town, and then a patrol car driven by a pal, Fred Cullen, will siren him and pull him over. My cop will be looking for a stolen Caddy that matches Simstead's. You keep going two or three miles, so he can't see you, then take an off ramp. Take one that also allows you to return south. We'll let him take up the chase, hoping he'll go north clear to Fresno. Give him five, maybe ten minutes and then get on the southbound freeway and on your way."

Kenderson stayed silent for several seconds, as he absorbed Fallon's plan. "Okay, but what if he follows me south?"

Fallon said, "Let's not cross that bridge until we come to it, okay?"

"Should I borrow my wife's Plymouth? It's newer and faster?"

"No, just do it like I said."

"Will the Washington's know I'm coming?"

"I'll let them know. So good luck and on your way." Fallon walked back to the unmarked car and quickly pulled away from the curb, leaving Kenderson with a whirlwind of conflicting feelings. So now he was supposed to follow a scheme that could risk his and Freddie's life. He rebelled against the idea of being a passive cog in a wheel, but reluctantly admitting he couldn't have thought of anything better, he climbed back in the Datsun and headed south for the Washington home.

After Fallon's comments about informants, he imagined one of the organization's goons on every lighted intersection he drove through. Well, hell that's part of the plan, he told himself. He parked half a block from the Washingtons and quickly walked to the front door and rang the bell. Nehi opened the door immediately. Freddie, holding a small bundle, stood behind him. "He's got his meds, some food and extra clothing. Thanks for acting fast."

Washington helped Freddie through the door, and after wishing them both luck, quickly closed it. "Follow me," Kenderson told his ward, and together they hurried to the Datsun and in a few moments had turned around, heading for the north bound freeway toward Fresno.

"We going north?"

"For now, okay?" Keep down as much as you can."

Freddie seemed fairly calm as he slipped down in the passenger seat. The northbound freeway was only a few blocks away and once on it, Kenderson speeded up. He was approaching the northern city limits when he spotted headlights on his tail. It was Simstead's Cadillac closing in behind him. He wished he had demanded Fallon let him have a faster car but it was too late now. He felt a rising panic. Where was Fallon's cop? What was to stop Simstead from simply shooting them both as he drove alongside? Simstead was almost even with the Datsun on the outside lane and waving at Kenderson to pull over. Warning Freddie to stay out of sight, the probation officer floored the accelerator and for a few seconds, drew ahead of the Cadillac.

Where in hell was the cop Fallon promised? Kenderson felt cold sweat on his forehead, his hands frozen on the steering wheel. In the rearview mirror, he saw Simstead pulling alongside, a revolver showing in his left hand. In desperation, he shouted, "Freddie, if the guy starts shooting, I'll slow down and you bail out. Find someplace to hide and let me know where you are." He thought, if I live through this.

Glancing to his left he saw Simstead aiming at the car and on impulse, hit the brakes and the Cadillac sped by. He looked for an off ramp but the midtown exit was at least two miles ahead. Simstead was slowing down, and horns blasting registered the ire of motorists who were unable to pass.

Relief flooded his whole body as he saw the flashing red and blue lights of a patrol car approaching in the rearview mirror. About time! He waited for the patrol car to red-light Simstead and pull him over to the emergency lane on the right. To his surprise, the police car swung in behind the Datsun, red lights flashing. What the hell is he pulling me over for? It's Simstead he wants. Wasn't the damn fool briefed correctly? Reluctantly, he pulled into the emergency lane and stopped the car. He could see the Caddy ahead, slowing down but continuing north. A black officer approached, ticket book in hand. Kenderson was about to explode when the big cop said, "I'm Fred Cullen. We had a change of plans."

"Like what?" Kenderson tried to conceal his wrath.

"Like letting Simstead see you taking the midtown off ramp leading to the city jail, with me behind you. He'll think we arrested Freddie. It will take time for him to find out we didn't. By then, you should be well on your way south. Turn right when you get off the ramp. There's no traffic on that side street. There's a couple of things I need to tell you."

"Okay. Simstead was about to start shooting."

"We know, but he's got a license for that gun. It's better this way and nobody gets hurt."

Kenderson started the car and pulled into the right lane, taking the midtown off ramp and then making a sharp right and pulling to the curb. The patrol car stopped in back of him. Cullen got out and approached the driver's side.

"Fallon says if you get into trouble, phone this number." He handed a slip of paper to Kenderson. "Let him know where you are, and he'll try to get some help from local cops in Kern county."

He pointed to the street running parallel to the freeway. "Stay on this street until you get to Union. Turn right and then your first left and you'll come to an on ramp going south. Good luck, and you, too, kid."

Freddie sat up in the seat, grinning. Kenderson thought for a moment he was going to wiseoff to the officer. Instead, he seemed downright cheerful after the confrontation with Simstead. To Kenderson, the strain was wearing him down and he fervently hoped once Freddie was safe, the pressure would ease up.

As he entered the southbound freeway, he felt relieved. He had Freddie look at the map Sarah MacCormick had given him, and tell him the name of the county road where he was to turn off.

"It's Pelican," Freddie said.

"Like the bird?"

"Yeah, the ones with long legs."

Traffic was light and with each mile, Kenderson felt better. It was a clear night with stars and a crescent moon above. Kenderson enjoyed the picture of Simstead cussing everyone around the police station, trying to get some answers about Freddie. And then it occurred to him that Setich had lots of cops on his payroll. One of them could have watched Fred Cullen's movements and figured out what happened. Suddenly tense, he began to watch the headlights behind him. Was one of them closing fast? He dug in his pocket and pulled out the slip of paper Cullen had given him and held it under the dash light. The area code was different, so it had to be in the Bakersfield area. The freeway signs indicated a number of small towns on either side of them. Should he turn off now and wait? He picked up his portable phone and, holding the wheel with one hand, keyed in the ten digit number and then punched the send button. The phone rang six times before a rough voice with a southern accent answered. "Hi, Al Fallon gave me this number to call. I'm not far from Pelican Road. I'm in a '72 Datsun. I'm not sure I'm being followed. But if I am, the guy in a new Cadillac is armed and determined to kill the boy with me and probably me, too. Can you help?"

"Ahm on Pelican, too. Iffen ah see a Caddy on you ass, I'll be right glad to be of service."

Kenderson felt a sudden urge to laugh. He managed a quick "thanks" and punched the end button. He laughed aloud from relief. Freddie halfheartedly joined in, not sure what had pleased his PO. Al Fallon, Kenderson decided, was a man for all seasons. The momentary glee died as he spotted headlights rushing from the rear. The pursuing car looked like the Caddy. Only a mad as hell Simstead would be driving like that. He floored the accelerator but was no match for the more powerful car. The sign rushing toward him said Pelican Road one mile. Hopefully, he could make the turn before Simstead caught up with him. Watching the rearview mirror, he confirmed it was Simstead on his tail. Did the man know where he planned to turn? Probably not. Taking another turnoff with Simstead on his tail would be suicide. He swerved abruptly into the right hand lane and slued onto the Pelican Road exit. The Datsun rocked and skidded but stayed upright. The Cadillac was too close to follow but Kenderson knew it would be a only a matter of minutes before the big goon would be in hot pursuit.

He drove as fast as he deemed safe on the two lane road. He glanced hopefully at several farm houses with lights in the windows. Did Fallon's friend live in one of these? He could see no car waiting in a driveway or alongside the road. He began to feel desperate. Without help, he and Freddie were doomed. He thought about abandoning the car and the two of them running into a field to hide in the darkness. That would buy some time. Unconsciously, his foot lightened on the gas pedal. He suddenly envisioned the solid looking detective watching him and with a shout, crunched the gas pedal to the floor boards. *Fallon had been as good as his word. This was not the time for doubts.*

They passed a packing shed and then a lighted corner store and gas pump. Nothing. Searching the rearview, he saw twin headlights enter Pelican Road and knew that it would be only a matter of minutes before Simstead caught them. He decided he should not turn right on County Road K1, which Sarah had indicated was where the Converse Ranch was located. It won't matter one way or another if Simstead catches up to us. He regretted not having asked Farber for a weapon, or at least borrowed one. He realized he didn't know which of his friends even owned a gun. How far to the next town and was there a police station? Where in hell was Fallon's friend? The map showed K1 about ten miles from the freeway offramp and he was sure they must be nearing it. The headlights revealed a picture of a stop sign in the middle of the road which told him he'd arrived at K1. He quickly switched off the headlights and cautiously turned left, the opposite direction from the Converse farm and after a hundred yards, pulled into a shallow gully alongside the road.

Freddie remained still and strangely silent. The boy must be scared but he said nothing. Kenderson turned in the seat and the boy did the same. Heart beating, he watched the intersection, praying that his move would confuse Simstead and give them a little breathing room. They watched in silence for what seemed a long time, and then they looked at one another questioningly. It was too dark to tell Freddie's exact expression but Kenderson believed it was the same as his own. Flat out relieved. They continued to observe the intersection in silence, which lasted until a pickup truck stopped and then drove on in the direction of the freeway.

Kenderson had no intention of driving anywhere until he was sure of Simstead's location. Had Fallon's friend caught up with Simstead? The answer came about a minute later. A sheriff's patrol car rolled up to the intersection and stopped. Behind the thick wire screen that separated the driver from the rear, sat a man who strongly resembled Curt Simstead. The confirmation came a few moments later when a deputy driving the Cadillac made the same stop. Kenderson and Freddie let out a simultaneous whoop and did a high five.

"Let's get you to the Converse's home right now."

Pulling out of the gully and making a U-turn, Kenderson drove south on K1 for roughly five miles, looking for the wooden arch with the Converse name Sarah had described. A small light illuminated the sign, making it easy to locate in the dark. Driving up the graveled entrance, Kenderson parked in front of a two story farm house that looked well maintained. A woman about Sarah's age hurried out to the car. She was smiling.

"Did you have a problem with the directions?"

"They were excellent. An incident I'll tell you about, held us up for a few minutes. This is Freddie Hawkins."

She smiled again. "Sarah has talked a lot about you both. Please come in."

Freddie looked fidgety. Time for his Ritalin. The boy had been remarkably cool through the frightening ordeal with Simstead. Kenderson silently wished he felt as composed as Freddie appeared.

Once inside, Arlene Converse insisted they have some cookies and soda or coffee. At her suggestion, Freddie went out to the car and returned with his small suitcase borrowed from Mary Washington.

"He needs to take his Ritalin. He's been through a lot of stress today." A glass of water was provided and Kenderson watched as Freddie took one of the small, white pills. Arlene insisted on showing Freddie his room. When she came down, she explained that her husband, Robert, was in Los Angeles making some purchases for the farm.

Kenderson knew he had to tell her what had happened. Freddie would be safe only as long as Simstead was in jail. He told her of the pursuit and the arrest. "It won't take long for someone in the organization to get him out on bail. They'll start looking for connections with the MacCormick family in this area. It's only a matter of time before they'll come looking for him."

He quickly sketched the circumstances behind their flight out of Oso County. Arlene was clearly upset.

"Can't anyone help? How about our county sheriff? He wouldn't be obligated to the officials in Oso County, would he?"

Kenderson agreed but right now, he had to find out how long Simstead would be in jail. Asking permission to use her phone, he was shown to a small office which she said her husband used for business accounts. Arlene seemed like a warm and caring person, a possible permanent placement sometime in the future, once the danger to the boy had ended.

He called several times before getting Fallon at home. "I'm at the Converses with Freddie. Thank you and your southern friend for the rescue. I thought we were goners."

Fallon laughed. "My friend Ernie told me it got pretty close. Sorry about that."

"Should I get Freddie out of here now? How long is our friend going to be locked up?"

Fallon laughed again. "Well, my deputy friend tells me the phone system has gone to hell and Mr. Simstead is just going to have to wait until tomorrow sometime late, before he can make that one phone call."

Kenderson found himself chuckling. "I'd like to leave the boy here overnight, maybe longer if it's safe. If Mr. Converse is anything like his wife, Freddie could fit in here. And it would be with relatives of his mother. He'd like that."

"I think he'll be safe for a day or two. So you'll be heading back to Santa Inglesia tonight?"

"Yes, my wife and kids are terribly frightened and they need me. Our old cat is missing and they wonder if Setich has killed her as a warning to us."

"He's capable of doing that."

"I'd like to meet with you tomorrow about noon at the Seven- Eleven. Freddie has begun to open up to me. He said he and Ermon were in the house at the time Hawkins was killed but the library door was closed and they weren't aware anything was wrong. The killer doesn't know about the boys being there. Maybe we can smoke out whoever it is, by letting that information hit the streets. Freddie would be in a safe place but we could be watching for the killer to show up at a false address."

Fallon sounded interested. "Let me run this by the Sergeant." He paused. "So far, noon tomorrow sounds fine."

"Good, and there's some more I need to tell you about why Setich wants to silence Freddie."

"Okay, unless you hear from me, I'll meet you at noon."

Kenderson felt an impulse to say, okay, partner, but he didn't. Cops, as a rule, didn't like social worker types. He couldn't count the times he'd heard cops say, "We catch the little bastards and lock their asses up and the next day you persuade the courts to turn 'em loose."

He hung up the phone and not finding the woman of the house, he mounted the stairs, letting them know he was coming. The bedroom door was open and he saw an exhausted Freddie lying on the bed and Arlene Converse sitting on the edge, gently stroking his hair. Freddie seemed relaxed and enjoying the attention, which was something Kenderson had never witnessed. His ward had always resented any kind of physical contact or show of affection. This was a kind of miracle, affected by a remarkable woman whose kindness and warmth were reaching a very suspicious sixteen year old who trusted no one since his mother's death.

Kenderson told the sleepy boy he was leaving, which earned a brief wave of the hand. Arlene Converse patted the boy on the arm and said she would be right back. She followed Kenderson down the stairs and into the living room. "You'll be back?" She asked.

"Yes, and soon. It's not the right time to say this, but I've never seen the boy respond to anyone like he has you." She smiled.

"He has no family now, except Sarah." He realized immediately she knew what he was hinting at.

"It's something Robert and I will talk about. But what happens now. Will he be safe?"

Kenderson filled her in on the information he'd learned from Fallon. "The man will be out of jail soon and it won't take the organization long to find out you're a relative. They'll come here looking for the boy. It could get rough. Fortunately, the local deputies seem to know their job and should be on the alert, once Simstead is out of jail." He paused. "I'm so sorry this had to happen." There was more he wanted to say, but for the moment he had to trust local law enforcement to protect this special lady.

Driving up the freeway on his way home, he suddenly felt dizzy and sick at the stomach, stress symptoms from dodging Simstead and possible death. His thoughts drifted back to Nam, remembering the constant fear of being hit by a mortar fragment or a bullet from a rapid fire weapon. This tension was different. In a firefight, he knew what he was supposed to do, keep the wounded guys alive until they made it to an aid station. Since Hawkins' murder, chaos had reigned. He had no plan or purpose to guide him. His only goal was to keep Freddie and his own family from harm. In a flash of clarity, he realized the danger would never end unless he, with help, resolved Hawkins' murder. He began to outline in his mind what he wanted to tell Fallon tomorrow.

It was almost midnight when he parked in the driveway. Fran looked strained as she opened the door and hugged him with an almost desperate embrace. "Why didn't you phone and let me know you were all right?"

Robert White

He held her outside and closed the front door. "Honey, for now we must assume everything is bugged. My portable, the house phones, even hidden mikes around the house. If we talk, it must be where we can use some covering noise, like the shower or TV."

She looked even more desperate and he feared she might fall apart under the pressure. "Honey, I'm going to ask Fallon to set up some kind of a trap for the killer and get this mess over with."

She didn't even ask what it was. "Let's go inside, I'm emotionally done in."

They undressed, sticking to innocuous matters like what the kids did in school that day. Unable to sleep, Kenderson went over one scenario after another in his mind. There had to be a way to force the killer to reveal himself. He somehow fell asleep and remembered scary dreams the next morning.

FRIDAY MORNING

The next morning, Kenderson was at odds with Fran about how much to tell Vernon and Cindy. Fran insisted, "Honey, they talk to their friends and to one another about what's going on. I don't see any way to change that."

"But can we do nothing to stop them from revealing information that may jeopardize someone's life, including their own? I don't want to panic them into thinking they're in immediate danger."

Fran's tone sharpened. "Aren't we all in immediate danger. If they steal our cat to scare us, what will they do next?"

"Okay, are you willing to let me talk to the kids?" Her brief nod revealed her ambivalence. "Some place where we can't be overheard." She nodded again.

Getting the kids into the backyard without a major debate wasn't easy. He silently shushed them, as each started to protest being pushed out the rear sliding doors. Once outside, he drew them close and said, "Last night, a goon who works for the Hawkins organization, now controlled by another criminal, Arnie Setich, tried to kill Freddie Hawkins and, I believe, me, too."

Vernon and Cindy listened openmouthed. Vernon started to talk but Fran put her hand on his shoulder. "Listen to your Dad."

"There's a lot of corruption in the city, and except for one
or two cops, we can't trust local law enforcement to protect us.
An attempt may be made to force me to reveal Freddie Hawkins' whereabouts by threats to hurt you. They may have taken
Bandit for starters. For now, we have to assume microphones
are in the house, the phones are bugged and the signal on the
cellular is compromised."

Cindy stared wide-eyed. "Like on TV spy movies?"

"Like on TV, except no hero is going to rescue us. We're
on our own. So assume anything you say in the house or on the
phone can be overheard." Feeling his usual guilt, he wanted to
apologize to them but refrained, deciding it would serve no
purpose. "I'm hoping, with help, this can be solved quickly.
That's it for now."

Vernon and Cindy were anxious to ask a lot of questions
but instead, walked quietly back into the house. Fran lingered
to say, "It was the right thing to do." They kissed warmly and
Kenderson followed her into the house and started directly to
the garage door.

"Breakfast?" Fran asked. Kenderson shook his head.

"I'll pick up a Danish later."

Entering the Datsun, his stomach burned, making him
wonder if he was getting an ulcer. Why not, everything else is
going to hell.

At the office, he found it hard to sit still long enough to
return phone calls from his wards and a few parents. Fallon had
told him the meet would be at noon at the Seven-Eleven, but
that was three hours away. He thought of phoning, but resisted.
I'll get him in trouble, if I don't cool it. The second call involved
one of his kids, Juan Morales, who was fighting at school and
facing suspension. He talked to the vice principal, assuring him
that he would warn Juan that any more trouble, he would be out
of the Diversion Program. He spent a few minutes conveying

Robert White

this information directly to the boy, who appeared to understand the gravity of the warning.

About midmorning, Washington got to work, immediately entering Kenderson's office and shutting the door. "So, how did it go last night?"

Kenderson's expression was grim. "Simstead almost caught us. But we got rescued by a cop friend of Fallon's. The Converse home would make a great placement, but I've got to get him out of there soon. It won't take Setich long to make the MacCormick connection and go after the boy."

He spared Washington the details. Their close call would only make him feel bad about insisting Freddie leave.

"So what's next?"

"I'm meeting Fallon at noon."

"You want me along?" Kenderson shook his head.

"I would appreciate your driving by the high school a couple of times today. I told the kids this morning what's been happening."

Washington said he would make several passes and contact Fallon if anyone who shouldn't be, was parked and watching. "What about Fran?"

"This is her morning in the office."

FRIDAY AFTERNOON

Fallon slid into Kenderson's Datsun and, for once, didn't comment on its condition. "My friend, Ernie, said you and your boy had a close call last night. Said he had trouble getting the patrol car started."

Kenderson shook his head. "We both sweated blood and I need a gun. If he'd found us where we'd parked in the dark alongside the road, he would have simply executed us. My boss could okay one but I can't tell him what's going on. As far as he's concerned Freddie is off our caseload and, therefore, no concern of his or the Center's."

Fallon was silent for a long moment before saying, "I've got a couple of spare pieces. You know how to shoot?"

"I had some training."

"Okay, but don't get caught with it. The serial number has been filed off and it's accurate at close range. I've got the piece in my trunk. I'll slip it to you with some extra ammo before we split." Kenderson had mixed feelings, when he thanked Fallon. Fran was opposed to guns in any way, shape or form. After telling Fallon he planned to move Freddie out soon, the detective said. "I agree. My friend tells me Simstead was bailed out late this morning by some hard-looking guy with dull grey eyes."

"That would be Arnie Setich."

"My friend also warned the both of them he would slam their asses in jail if they came in the county again. That should hold them for a day or two, but the boy should be gone by tomorrow."

"Any ideas where I can hide him until this gets cleaned up?"

Fallon pondered for a moment, and then said, "He can stay with a relative for a few days. But I won't tell you who or where. Okay with you?"

Kenderson nodded. "About setting a trap for the killer, can I tell you what I think might work?"

Fallon looked doubtful but grunted for Kenderson to go ahead.

"Setich and Pete want Freddie dead, as far as I can figure, because he recently discovered they either force fed his mother the altered sleeping pills with a fatal quantity of codeine, or substituted them for her regular ones. Hawkins, of course, ordered her death because she was threatening to go to the Attorney General in Sacramento."

"I'm following you, so what's the gig, and who do you hope to flush out?"

"Freddie and his buddy, Ermon, were in the mansion during the hours Hawkins was killed. Nobody knows that except the boys and you and me. Freddie finally told me this but, he has no idea what happened or who was in the mansion at the time. He and Ermon were blasting their ears off in his room, listening to "Eternal Dead" or one of those groups. The killer doesn't know the boys were there. If he learns they were, he won't know whether or not the two saw or heard something that would incriminate him. He will be anxious to shut Freddie up permanently."

"I get your drift. Is this one of your social work techniques?" He laughed to show he was kidding, but Kenderson didn't join in.

"Once the word is out, Setich will send Simstead to the Center. But what I'm hoping is that somebody we don't suspect will show up. It's dangerous. But I believe Hawkins' killing was triggered by some new enterprise the organization was planning. If we catch the killer, I believe it will bring them all down."

Fallon fell silent, mulling over the proposal.

"So both Sarah and the boy would be out of the picture, right?"

"Absolutely."

"And where would we set up the trap?"

"The Diversion Center has a couple of furnished rooms with beds and washing facilities where kids can stay overnight."

"So how does the word get out?"

Kenderson grinned. "That's your department. You have informants, and information can go both ways, right?"

Fallon mulled that over. "Okay, can do."

"How long after the word gets out, will somebody act?"

"About five minutes after I tell my snitch and warn him it's confidential stuff and not to blab it around."

"Good deal. Maybe tomorrow?" Fallon looked doubtful.

"Might be too late. You want me to phone Ernie that you'll be coming to the Converses today?"

"You're right, I shouldn't wait until Simstead starts trailing me again. I'll leave right now. Maybe your friend can let the Converses know I'm coming. I don't think my phone is secure."

Fallon nodded and went to the rear of his car. Opening the trunk, he fished a small canvas bag containing a thirty-eight Smith and Wesson revolver from a side pocket and moved swiftly back to the driver's side of the Datsun. He looked around and seeing no one, passed the bag to Kenderson. "Hope you don't have to use it. I'll have Ernie see you and the boy get out of the county in one piece." Kenderson thanked him and Fallon added, "When you get back here, phone me. I'll tell you where to drop the boy."

"One more thing. Can you change cars?"

"I was thinking the same thing. I'll switch with Fran."

Kenderson waited until Fallon was out of sight before driving out of the parking lot and heading north toward the Oso County Court House. Fortunately, the dispatcher knew him and it took only a few minutes to drive up the ramp to the parking spaces reserved for county workers. He wrote a note to Fran, telling her he'd explain the need to switch. Fran carried a set of keys to the Datsun so there was no need to leave his. He waved his thanks to the dispatcher as he drove the Plymouth through the barrier and headed east in the direction of the southbound freeway. Four different times, he turned right off Kensington Boulevard and parked, watching to see if he was being followed. Finally, satisfied nobody was trailing him, he entered the southbound off ramp and drove steadily at 55 miles an hour, staying in the right-hand lane, watching the rearview to see if he was being followed.

On reaching Pelican Road, he drove until he reached the crossroad stop sign at County Road K1. Still alert to being watched or followed, he continued on Pelican for another three miles. When he saw no sign of pursuit, he turned into a farmhouse driveway on the left side of the road, backed out and returned to K1.

He parked in the circular driveway and mounted the stairs. He felt his heart beating faster as he rang the bell. He heard the chimes and silently hoped everyone was safe. After a delay, a tall, slightly graying man wearing jeans and a white sports shirt, opened the door. "I'm Robert Converse. We've been waiting since Ernie phoned you'd be coming. Please come in."

He'd expected, at the very least, an angry rebuke for placing the man's family at risk. They shook hands. Kenderson found himself admiring the man's quiet confidence. He was a good match for Arlene Converse.

Robert went to the foot of the stairs and called, "It's all right, it's Mr. Kenderson."

A moment later Arlene, dressed simply like her husband, came down the stairs behind Freddie. Kenderson could feel the growing bond between Arlene and the boy from the way they looked at one another. Freddie showed his unhappiness at having to leave, but his reaction was a far cry from his former responses, which would have been an unending string of four letter words. Kenderson found himself hoping again that Freddie might eventually find a permanent home with these exceptional people. The parting was brief.

"Freddie will be safe. I cannot tell you where or with whom. I won't know either. When the danger is over, I'll be in touch. We'd better go now." He shook hands with both of them. Freddie gathered his few belongings, walked to the car and entered the passenger side. With a brief wave from both, Kenderson drove to the county road and turned left.

Freddie was silent and Kenderson could tell he hated leaving the Converses. Kenderson said, "When this is over, maybe you can go back. Both Mr. and Mrs. Converse liked you and I'm guessing you like them, too." Freddie grunted, too unhappy to share the wrench of departing. About thirty miles from Santa Inglesia, his cellular buzzed. It startled him, wondering who couldn't wait until he got back to the office or his home. He pressed the on button and heard Fallon's voice. It was difficult to hear him because of the static. He pulled out his aerial, which helped some. Fallon was saying, "Meet me at

Fowlers Inn. It's just after you cross the county line. I'll pick up your cargo there, okay?"

Kenderson started to question the location, but Fallon abruptly cut him off. "See you there." The dial tone came on.

Kenderson felt his hands grow sweaty. Did the call mean Simstead was looking for them in Santa Inglesia? He guessed Fallon was making sure Simstead would be nowhere around when he picked up Freddie. In fifteen minutes they saw the tall Texaco Gas sign that marked the Fowler Inn, and several other gas stations and eateries located a few miles ahead. Pulling off the freeway, he headed for the parking lot next to the Inn. Stopping the motor, he put a restraining hand on Freddie until he'd had a chance to locate Fallon's car. He watched for five minutes while a dozen cars stopped at the gas pumps or parked next to the Inn. He began to wonder if Fallon had really made the call and was feeling increasingly nervous when he heard the cop's voice behind him.

"Don't look around." He spoke quietly. "Freddie, slip out the door and keep low. I'm going to pull in back of the Plymouth and stop. Stay down and get in as quick as you can."

Kenderson watched as Fallon moved to the gas pump behind them, quickly pulling out the hose and replacing it against the dispensing tank. He had lost sight of the car after it pulled away, but a minute later he saw the Honda directly behind the Plymouth. "Go for it, Freddie," he said, "I'll be in touch."

Moving quickly, the boy slipped out of the seat and into the open rear door of Fallon's car. In a matter of seconds, the Honda was gone. Kenderson still did not turn around but a minute later, started the Plymouth and backing out, headed for the freeway. Northbound, he felt a sense of relief that Freddie was safe but thinking of the dangers and fearful tasks that lay ahead, his peace of mind didn't last.

Robert White

He anxiously wondered if his idea of luring Hawkins' killer into the open would work. Maybe Hawkins' killer was really Setich or Pete. Their alibis were questionable but there was no way to prove they were false unless someone would contradict their stories. That was unlikely. Could Simstead have gained access to the office and caught Hawkins' off guard? Kenderson's impression was that Simstead was an enforcer and normally would have no direct dealings with the big boss. But that was an assumption, and he wondered if Castro or anyone had checked out the man's alibi. He made a mental note to ask Fallon if anyone had checked Simstead's whereabouts last Sunday.

As he parked in his usual space at the Center, he saw with relief that Farber was getting in his car ready to leave. Marilyn said he was on his way to an after school speech to high school teachers and administrators.

"Trying to drum up business?"

Marilyn teased, "You don't want any more cases?"

He grinned,"Not right now, thanks."

Inside his office he sat down heavily and realized he felt like an emotional dish rag. He took out of sheet of paper and wrote: Are the kids and Fran okay? Are the Washington's okay? What about Edward Nichol's alibi? Is Bandit back home? He pondered the next question, which was probably the most important one. How quick can we set up the trap to lure Hawkins' killer into the open?

The phone rang but when he held it to his ear, he had difficulty understanding who was speaking because of stressful tears. "Daddy, daddy." It was Cindy. He felt his face flush. What had happened? His throat, constricted with fear, blocked his speech for a moment.

"Yes, it's me."

"They cut off the end of Bandit's tail. She keeps crying. Oh, Daddy it's awful."

He knew he had to bring her back to reality and give her some concrete instructions. "Honey, listen to me. Is she bleeding?"

"Just a little."

"Then put some peroxide on her tail so it won't get infected. Can you do that? If she's still bleeding put a bandage on with some tape. Can you do that?" He wanted to ask if Vernon was there but didn't. It was important Cindy deal with this herself.

She seemed to be calming down and the sobs lessening. "I'll be home soon. Where's your Mom?"

"She's over at the Washington's. She doesn't know about it."

"You take care of Bandit, okay? I'll be home in a few minutes."

"Okay, I'll do what you say."

Replacing the phone, he felt deflated. They should just get the hell out of Santa Inglesia before they were all killed like the Condon family. Fallon could protect Freddie and Sarah. There were plenty of social work jobs in California in the juvenile justice field. He felt a vast relief, visualizing the peace and security he and the family would find in another city. The Diversion Program had seemed like the answer to his prayers, for an opportunity to change lives. But he hadn't counted on this scenario of horror. And beyond Castro and Fallon, he had no real help. He shied away from talking to Nehi and Mary about what was happening. Why embroil them more? They would be lucky if the organization didn't exact some retribution for keeping Freddie overnight. His anxiety grew.

He hurriedly phoned home, and this time Vernon answered. He asked for Fran but she still wasn't home. He asked if Bandit was okay and Vernon assured him the cat had a white bandage on it's tail and no longer seemed to be hurting. He felt an urge to blurt out his fears to Vernon, but realized he had to get himself under control before he did something stupid and irreversible. Kenderson hung up after telling Vernon he'd be right home. He wished he could talk to Fallon but he knew the detective was busy making sure his ward was safe. He must fight his own panic. He couldn't help anyone if he let blind fear dictate his actions. It was time for reason to take charge.

Going over the past days, he reminded himself he'd stayed in charge when the situation with Simstead was menacing. Even when Fallon wasn't around. It dawned on him that much of his panic was simply lack of sleep. I ought to be able to take care of that right now. He started to leave, then remembered he couldn't phone Fallon from home. He sat down again and dialed the number the detective had given him. He got the answering service and said, "Put out the word on Freddie tonight. Say he'll be sleeping at the Diversion Center, arriving there about nine o'clock tomorrow night. That he's thinking of turning himself in. It will be dark by then and, hopefully, make whoever wants him dead feel safer. I hope that will be enough time for your informant to pass the word. If I don't hear from you, I'll meet you at the Center about eight thirty tomorrow. If it's no go, phone me at home and tell me your son is in trouble again." He hung up the phone and, wondering if he'd covered all the bases, rose to leave. He was too tired to think any more, so he told Marilyn he was through for the day and walked out of the Center to Fran's Plymouth. As he drove home, he checked the rearview mirror to see if he was being followed.

Fran looked scared when she came into the garage to greet him. "Is it safe to talk here?" Kenderson nodded.

"Cindy phoned you about Bandit?" He nodded again. "What are we going to do? I'm scared for all of us."

Kenderson hugged her. She nestled her head on his shoulder. "I'm scared, too. After Cindy phoned about what they'd done to Bandit, all I could think of was moving out of Santa Inglesia before it was too late."

Fran brightened. "Right now, that sounds good to me. I'm not sure how much longer I can take this pressure."

"Don't laugh, but the first thing I need is sleep. I'm so exhausted I can't think straight. And I need to have my wits about me. Fallon and I have a plan to lure Hawkins' killer into showing himself. There's little risk. The worst that can happen, it won't work."

Fran shook her head. "What makes you think it will work?"

"Because the bait will be Freddie. Only he won't be there."

He quickly described the plan and the events of the past three days. "If they wanted to kill us, they could have. Why didn't they? My guess is, Phil Hawkins has convinced Setich he can get the same results quicker and without bad publicity. I don't know what the end results will be, but I don't think we have much time." They walked into the kitchen and the conversation became safe and mundane.

Fran had prepared an early dinner of broiled steak and yams, which was one of Kenderson's favorites. But tonight he might as well have been eating cardboard. He was totally used up and sleep was the only solution. After signaling the others to follow his lead, Kenderson shifted from what happened at school to Bandit's mutilation. "I don't know how she got out of the yard. She's too old to climb the fence. And her tail looks like she got caught in a lawnmower."

Robert White

Raised eyebrows greeted his remarks, but everyone went along, verbally agreeing that must be the answer. Kenderson thought, if Setich and his goons were listening, they'd be disappointed. Soon afterward, he took a shower and was in bed by eight thirty. Fran gave him one of her sleeping pills which helped him drop into a deep sleep.

SATURDAY MORNING/AFTERNOON

Kenderson hoped the long sleep would invigorate him but it had the opposite effect. He woke up at eight thirty feeling groggy and with Fran's urging, he forced himself to finish a small omelet and piece of toast. The coffee helped some. He tried to plan the day, but found himself confused about what he should do first. He told himself to quit stalling but that didn't help either. Deep in his guts, he admitted he hated facing what was ahead. The idea of jumping in the car with the family and leaving Santa Inglesia forever seemed more attractive than ever. He thought how pleased Fran would be if they really did leave. But there were some good reasons to stay, he reminded himself. If they were lucky, he and Fallon could get a good look at whoever responded to the news that Freddie Hawkins was sleeping in the Diversion Center building.

Making sure the kids and Fran were not around, he slipped out to the car and pulled the canvas bag out of the glove compartment to examine the thirty-eight Fallon had lent him. The incongruity of possessing a weapon struck him. Hey, I'm no cop, my mission is to help pre-delinquent kids stay out of the juvenile justice system. A gun is for protection. If we see the guy tonight and he starts shooting, am I supposed to shoot back? Use of firearms was not taught at the School of Social Welfare at UC Berkeley. He felt a twinkling of humor, thinking how some of his former professors would react, seeing him with a gun in his hand. He slipped the revolver back into the bag, opened the trunk, hid the weapon under some old sweaters and then returned to the kitchen.

Fran came in and said Nehi and Mary were dropping by later in the morning. "I had to be careful what I said and was awfully abrupt with her. I'll have to explain when they get here."

"Did they say why they were coming?

Fran shook her head. "Maybe it was something they didn't want to mention over the phone."

A short time later, Nehi and Mary arrived. The day was comfortable and Kenderson suggested they talk out on the patio. Once there, Washington asked if Freddie was safe. "Mary's been raking me over the coals for insisting Freddie leave our house. I'll feel like hell if my overprotectiveness got either of you in a jam."

Kenderson glanced at Fran, asking her silently if he should tell what had happened after he'd taken Freddie from the Washington's home. Her shoulder shrug told him it was his call.

"We did run into some problems with Simstead but we survived. I hesitate to tell you more because if you don't know anything about Freddie Hawkins, you'll both be safer. Let me say he's under protection but where, I don't know."

Both Nehi and Mary expressed relief. Mary added, "I liked the boy and that was a surprise. His reputation for a long time has been of a selfish little monster." She turned to Kenderson with a smile. "Are you by any chance reforming him?"

It was Kenderson's turn to grin. "Fat chance of that. Whatever impression I made was by accident and serendipity. He's beginning to think maybe for a social worker, I'm slightly okay." His tone turned serious.

Robert White

"I must tell you this quickly. We think the house, our phones, even the cellular one, is bugged. That's why we're sitting out here and why Fran was short with you, Mary."

"I thought something must be wrong. We usually wear out the phone line with chit chat about our husbands and kids."

Washington asked, "Are you in danger?"

Kenderson weighed whether to talk about Bandit's mutilation but didn't. "I think there is a temporary truce, at least an hiatus, while Phil Hawkins, who wants to avoid negative publicity this close to election, negotiates with Arnie Setich. Phil admitted to me he can only do business with his father's former enforcer on a strictly quid pro quo basis. Like, I'll give you this when I'm elected, if you don't louse things up by killing everyone you think is a threat now."

Washington sighed. "Phil is, at least halfway, in Arnie's pocket?"

"I guess. I don't claim to know all the angles to what's going on. Only that Hawkins' death has triggered a lot of heat and threats. It looks like the only way to stop this madness is to find Hawkins' killer."

Fran said, "I just want to get the hell out of here while we're in one piece."

"I agree with her,"Kenderson said, "and unless there is a break soon we can't sit around being clay pigeons."

Washington said, "You're not telling us everything, are you?"

"No we're not and for a good reason."

Fran added, "Jay's in over his head. He's carrying a gun for god's sake." Kenderson sighed. He hadn't done a good enough job at concealment.

Washington's reaction was immediate. "I carry a gun and I'm trained to use it." He paused, "I'm guessing you and Al Fallon are cooking something up. If I can help, say the word."

"Thanks and I'll remember that. But you and Mary have already done enough, and there is no use putting your lives on the line. If we get in a bind, your phone will ring."

"Good enough."

The Washingtons left soon after and Fran faced her husband. "So what are you and Al cooking up?"

"I told you. I'm hoping tonight we can narrow the search for Hawkins' killer. Please, let it go at that. If this so called truce ends, God knows what lengths Setich will go to find Freddie. I just don't want you to know more than you have to."

Her expression told him she was feeling helpless and angry because she wasn't involved in solving the family's problem.

The buzzing of his cellular made them both tense. He answered and held his breath. It was Fallon who simply said, "It's on." The curt message meant he was to meet Fallon at the Diversion Center around eight-thirty. "That was Fallon. It's on." Fran shook her head and went back into the house. He hated leaving her out but good sense said it was foolish to put her at further risk if it wasn't necessary.

He glanced at his watch. It was only eleven o'clock. Waiting for the night rendezvous was going to be a bitch on his nerves. He looked around the yard for a project, until it dawned on him that he'd totally neglected his other cases the past week and now was a good time to make home calls. He realized his workbook was still at the office. He called through the door to Fran, telling her what he was planning to do. She came out, looking unhappy. "I know that you're doing everything you can and I shouldn't get pissed, but I do. So mark it down to wifely bitchiness and go see your kids." He gave her a quick hug, grateful she was willing to say what was on her mind.

Starting the car and pulling onto the street, he watched the rearview carefully but no one seemed interested in his vintage Datsun. He parked near the Diversion Center entrance and using his key, quickly retrieved his black workbook and returned to his car. He thumbed through the fifteen names and selected Juan Morales, who lived on the edge of the Meadows. The boy's father had a good job working for a company which supplied chemicals and other equipment to swimming pool owners. A devoted father, Jorge and his wife, Francesca, were mortified that their oldest son had run afoul of the law. Strict church goers, they were baffled that Juan had been caught stealing. Fighting in school was bad, but stealing, Madre de Dios, it brought the greatest shame to the family name.

Mr. Morales, who was working in the front yard, came to the car when Kenderson parked in front of the house. He politely asked if Kenderson would like a beer and when the latter politely refused, he began to talk about Juan. "The kids don't have to work hard like I did. They expect everything to be done for them. My wife, she spoils Juan and I tell her he's got to learn to work if he's going to have his own family some day."

Juan was not home, which also troubled Mr. Morales. "I'll tell him you came by, Mr. Kenderson, and I'll tell him you said to not be stealing and fighting no more."

Good enough, Kenderson thought. Mr. Morales was a conscientious father who cared what happened to his children.

He thought of phoning Phil Hawkins and decided Phil had trouble enough dealing with Arnie Setich, and any questions Kenderson would ask would be answered in his usual vague, disjointed way.

He visited three more of his case families, only one of whom was home. By four o'clock, he had heard the world views of several parents, followed by hopes that Mr. Kenderson would, somehow, make their offspring attend school and keep them from becoming career criminals.

He returned home to find his family sitting around the glass topped table in the patio. He joined them, hoping the expressions he saw on their faces were from boredom, not anxiety. The day being pleasant and warm, Fran suggested eating out of doors, which everyone agreed to. Vernon and Cindy complained they were tired of going to pay phones to connect with their friends. Kenderson told them he hoped the crisis would soon be over. He discovered he was beginning to doubt tonight's trap plan would amount to anything, which made him feel depressed. My god, it has to end sometime. Let it happen before I'm ready for therapy myself.

Dinner was hot dogs and sauerkraut which was good late summer fare. He kept glancing at his watch and wondering if he could bear his anxieties for another two hours. The kids took off after eating and Kenderson and Fran sat in silence for a long time. The sunset was spectacular through the filmy clouds on the western horizon but neither mentioned it. The tension was palpable and Kenderson rose, feeling relieved because he had to prepare for the rendezvous and hoping Fran, with her unspoken unhappiness, would understand his need to leave.

SATURDAY EVENING

He debated whether he should even take the thirty-eight with him. Remembering Simstead's relentless pursuit which could have ended in his and Freddie's death, he decided discomfort with guns was not as bad as the discomfort of becoming a corpse. Besides, the truce between Phil and Arnie Setich could end at any time. Nobody would be safe then.

It was nearly dark when he parked on the street, one block from the center. Walking slowly, he passed the Victorian building twice before moving quickly to the front door and opening it with his ready key. Inside, he moved to his office and using a small flashlight, rewound the voice mail tape for messages. There were none and he moved to the staircase and mounted the stairs using the flash as a guide. The two dormitory rooms were to the right of the landing and, moving cautiously, he pushed the door open to the nearest one and entered. "You're late." Kenderson jumped and felt his whole body go cold. "Stay easy, man, it's just me."

"Fallon, you son of a bitch. You want to give me heart failure?" The beam of the flash illuminated Al Fallon's grinning face. He was sitting on the nearest single bed.

"How did you get in?"

"I'm a resourceful cop."

"So where do we wait for our guest? Here? If he's going to kill the kid, he'll probably open the door and start shooting."

"So we'll make a nice Freddie-size dummy in this bed and wait." Fallon took the pillows off the second bed and slid them under the covers of the first one. He pulled the sheets high so the gunman would believe the victim's head was hidden underneath.

"I locked the front door. How will he get in?"

"Like I did. With a lock pick."

"We'll wait in here?"

"Why not? We won't run the risk of losing him. I'm hoping there won't be any need for shooting."

"If it's Simstead, there'll be shooting."

"Let's wait and see. Where's the light switch, near the door?

Kenderson grunted an assent. "So shall I stand by the switch?"

"Too risky. We both have flashes. Mine will blind him for a moment and I can take him down and cuff him. But let's wait and see what he does. Let's get behind the other bed and wait. That's what detectives do a lot, and it's the worst part of the job."

The waiting was easy at first, but without air conditioning, the small room quickly became warm. He felt the sweat under his arms and crotch. He glanced at the illuminated dial. It was twenty minutes past nine. Was this a washout? Fallon had said little after his first alarming words. Kenderson's eyes gradually became accustomed to the growing darkness. Would they be able to hear sounds before the unknown walked into the room? Every five minutes, Kenderson looked at his watch. Time seemed to have stopped and the sweat stood out on his forehead. Why didn't they try to open one of the windows and let in a little air. He whispered this to Fallon who looked around. "There's no windows in this room, thought you'd know that."

Shit, what was he doing here, anyway? The idea seemed stupid now. Whoever it was, couldn't be so dumb as to believe Freddie Hawkins would actually be in the Diversion Center without any protection, just waiting to be shot dead. Nobody but a damn fool would buy that scenario. He suddenly felt Fallon's grip on his arm.

"Somebody's coming," He whispered. "Be cool, wait until I make a move."

Kenderson could hear the faint footfalls on the stair treads. Heart pounding, he inwardly exulted, the guy had really bought it. The intruder had reached the landing and from the hesitation, must be wondering in which wing the overnight rooms were located. Along the opposite corridor was a single office with the other bedrooms used for storage. The footsteps receded. The guy was exploring the other corridor. He'd have to be using a flashlight they'd see when he approached the door. What if there was shooting? He reached for his weapon but his hand came away empty. Christ, he'd left the thirty-eight in the car trunk. Suddenly, he felt cold steel being thrust in his hand. "Thought it might slip your mind. Same weapon as the other. Wait until I make a move, okay?"

Kenderson found himself holding his breath. His heart raced as the steps became audible again. He felt Fallon's restraining hand on his arm. "Stay cool."

He could see the wavering beam of the flash as its rays probed the bedroom door. Another hesitation by the intruder. Kenderson was suddenly aware he'd stopped sweating and was ice cold. The doorknob was turning, and a moment later the flash went off and the door opened ever so slowly. A dark figure neared the bed. Kenderson held his breath, waiting for the explosions that must come. Nothing happened for several moments and then he heard a voice that sounded familiar. "Freddie, Freddie, hey kid wake up, I want to talk to you."

Kenderson put a restraining hand on Fallon's arm. He needed to hear what Pete Hawkins wanted to ask his adoptive brother. He could hear the bed shaking and Pete's anger rising. "For Christ's sake wake up, you lazy little shit. I ain't got all night." The shaking made the springs squeak. Suddenly Pete got the idea. "Pillows! What kind of shit is this?"

Fallon's powerful flashlight beam illuminated Pete Hawkins' eyes and he threw his hands in front of his face. "Hey, don't shoot, I got no gun."

"Get your hands over your head and no quick moves. I'm going to turn on the lights now. So be cool and nobody gets hurt."

A bewildered Pete stood next to the bed, his hands high in the air. When his eyes adjusted to the light, he looked at Kenderson, surprise showing on his face. "So what the hell is this all about? All I wanted to do is talk to the kid and try to keep him from fucking up and getting hurt."

Kenderson weighed talking about Clarissa MacCormick's sudden death but decided to let Pete do the talking. Fallon was expertly patting him down for weapons. He looked at Kenderson. "He's clean."

"Pete, who sent you? And what do you want from Freddie? The last time your people showed an interest, was to end his life."

Pete shrugged. "I know. And I...we don't want that to happen."

"What's changed?"

"Shit, I don't have to talk to you none. I just want to see the kid. Where you got him stashed."

"I would need more information before I'd agree to your seeing him. Did Phil send you? Is he trying to buy Freddie's silence about what you and Arnie did to his mother?"

Pete looked deflated. "So the little shit talked to you. He's wrong, we never offed his mother on pills."

"Did I say pills?"

"Phil just wants the rough stuff to stop."

"At least until after the elections?"

"Nah, he never could stomach having to lean on the merchants."

"You mean beat and kill them."

Fallon sat on the edge of the bed, trying to hide his impatience, asked, "Is this a therapy session? If so, wake me up when it's over."

Kenderson felt irritated and turning to Fallon, "Anything you want to ask?"

Pete eyed Fallon suspiciously. "You the ass hole who broke in the West Office?"

"Not me. I'm here at the request of Mr. Kenderson. Other than that, I have no interest in what you and your cronies do."

Kenderson saw from Pete's smirk he wasn't buying Fallon's words. He wondered what else to ask Pete, but realized it didn't matter because the swarthy brother had said all he intended to.

"You going to arrest me for trespass?"

"Not me," Fallon said. "You want to bust him, Jay?"

Kenderson shook his head. He felt let down. A stressful night ended with nothing to show for the effort. He suddenly wondered how Setich and Pete intended to keep Freddie from talking about his mother's murder, short of killing him. Nothing like asking. "Pete, say Freddie agreed never to talk about his suspicions. What guarantee would you want that he'd stick to his word?"

Pete looked baffled. Evidently he'd never thought about it. Now the guy's here, Kenderson thought, why not pump him for information. He might reveal something without knowing he'd done it. He glanced at Fallon, who momentarily shifted his vigilance from Pete. Kenderson went on, "Pete, as long as you're here, who do you think killed your father?"

The question made him frown. "Asshole Freddie, who else. The kid lost it, plain and simple."

"But what if he didn't do it. Who else would want your Dad out of the way? How about you or Arnie?"

He bristled, "It wasn't us."

"But the word is you hated him because he favored Phil and treated you like a gofer."

"So, I'm not sorry to see that mean son of a bitch dead, but neither me nor Arnie had a hand in it."

"If it wasn't Freddie, who else wanted him out of the way?"

"How the fuck should I know."

"I want you to think about it. I know busting you for trespassing is small time, but it might make the Attorney General's office in Sacramento curious. They've been eyeing your operation for some time now, and Arnie would be highly pissed with you." Kenderson hoped that was true.

Pete squirmed. The subject was getting too close to home and he'd never acted as the spokesman for the organization.

"Pete, think. The organization plans to expand. The word gets out somehow, and the next thing your Dad is dead. What's the connection?"

"How the fuck should I know."

"And while we're talking about it, why beat up on Sarah MacCormick? What does she know that scares you people. Did she overhear something about the plans? Or were you afraid she'd go to the cops?

Out of the corner of his eye, he saw Fallon's agitation growing. The cop looked like he wanted to kill Pete. Kenderson, hoping he could calm the waters, asked, "Was it you who beat up Sarah?"

Pete, taking in Fallon's murderous look, hastily disclaimed having any part in her battering.

"Not me, it was Simstead. He went too far. We just wanted to scare her into keeping quiet."

Fallon didn't look like he was buying Pete's story but he kept himself under control.

Kenderson went on, "Did your expansion plan make somebody mad? Were you moving in on someone else's territory?"

Pete opened his mouth but Kenderson beat him to it. "I know, how the fuck should you know."

"But Pete, you have to agree that the expansion, whatever it is, ended in your Dad's being murdered. Could Phil have done it?"

Pete's face flushed. Kenderson wondered if he'd hit the bulls eye. "Are you saying it could be true?"

"Nah, they were asshole buddies. In Dad's eyes, Phil could do no wrong. And Phil thought the old man was tops."

"But you got red when I mentioned the possibility. Did they have a fight or disagreement before he was killed?"

"There was some yelling back and forth but it didn't mean nothing."

"Disagreement about the expansion plan?"

Pete, realizing he'd talked too much, remained silent. Kenderson looked at Fallon, who shrugged his shoulders. "Okay, Pete, take off. Tell whoever sent you, there's no deal. Freddie stays out of sight until we can be sure you won't be gunning for him."

Glancing over his shoulder to see if he was really safe, Pete scurried out of the room and his rapid footfalls on the stairs indicated he was leaving the Center at full bore.

Kenderson turned to Fallon. "He turned red. How come? He said there was a disagreement."

Fallon looked doubtful. "I've lived here since I was a kid. The old man never missed a game Phil played in. If you said a word against his old man, you'd have to fight Phil. Phil was mostly cool but when somebody missed a block or dropped a catchable pass, he'd chew on the guy's ass like you wouldn't believe."

Kenderson grew thoughtful. "There are people who deify someone they look up to, but these worshipful feelings can turn to hate in a flash. Maybe murder. I wonder if something about the expansion plagued Phil."

Fallon shrugged, "That's your line of work. Let's get the hell out of this hot box."

"Pete now knows you're helping me and Freddie. Will that put you in a bad space?"

"No more than usual. I don't think it's been any secret that Castro and his squad are not admirers of the Hawkins' organization or anybody in it."

"So we've checked the hell out of everybody's alibi. What about Phil's? Was he at the Elks Club when he claimed he was?"

Fallon shifted uncomfortably. "I think we just took his word about where he was. We can double check."

"I belong to the Elks. Let me do a little snooping."

Fallon nodded. "Before you get yourself in a jam, let's not forget Reverend Nichols."

"Nichols? What about him?

"We got his rap sheet. He wrecked hell out of one guy and another died after the beating he got from Nichols. He was charged, but never convicted."

"How come he got off?"

We had to go back to the original court documents. He claimed self defense. Said the two guys were blackmailing him and when he refused to pay, they tried to kill him."

"Do you know what they were holding over him?"

Fallon grinned, "He was fucking some other reverend's wife."

"Is this the righteous truth?" He paused for a moment, "What does Castro think?"

"The guy's a suspect."

Kenderson suddenly felt like a heavy load had been lifted off his back. If Nichols was the murderer, the threats and violence would mercifully stop. Or would that really happen? There were so many unresolved issues. Would the organization stop trying to kill Freddie or silence Sarah?

Fallon's voice broke his concentration. "You meditating? If not, let's get the hell out of here."

"You're right."

The hall wasn't much cooler than the small bedroom but once outside the building, the evening breeze refreshed them. Walking to their cars, Kenderson asked, "So what about Nichols. Does his alibi check out?"

"No, it doesn't. He says he was alone at the church preparing for the evening service. But nobody saw him there. So he's a suspect until he can come up with proof of where he was."

"So Setich and Pete have alibis. But Simstead?"

"I got around to talking to that arrogant bastard. He says he was in bed with his bimbo."

"And?"

"She says he was."

"So who's left?"

"Phil, which is too bad. He's the only one who acts like a law abiding citizen."

"Law abiding citizens kill people sometimes, right?"

"Right, and he's a politician."

"So will you check with Bill Foster and see if Phil was at his house at five-thirty, as he claimed. I'll ask about Sunday afternoon at the Elks Club."

Fallon said he would, and the two parted.

Hearing the garage door open, Fran hurried through the kitchen door to meet her husband. "So what happened? I've been a nervous wreck since you left."

"Pete came. He was unarmed and said all he wanted was to get assurances from Freddie he wouldn't talk about how his mother died."

"And you believed him?"

"As a matter of fact I did, and so did Fallon. Phil, who's all for keeping peace, must have put him up to it."

"But how can you deal with murderers? You could never trust Arnie Setich to keep his word."

"That's right but I'm trying to avoid a confrontation. Fallon has obtained further evidence on Nichols. He may be our killer."

Fran's dubious expression said she wasn't buying. "Com'on Jay, be serious. Reverend Nichols?"

"Yes, he's been violent in the past. But he's not the only suspect. Phil Hawkins may have killed his father over a disagreement about the expansion project."

She shook her head. "Is Mother Teresa on your suspect list?"

Robert White

Kenderson's evening had been stressful enough. More, he did not need. "Honey, let's cool it for tonight. I'm still beat from the waiting. The bedroom was sweltering."

Fran nodded, turned and walked into the kitchen. Kenderson followed and once inside, the conversation turned innocuous. They watched the ten o'clock news in silence and then, exchanging a few words about the next day's plans, went to their bedroom, Fran to read, Kenderson to try to make sense out of the conflicting thoughts racing through his brain. Both of them unconsciously waited for the relieving sounds of Vernon and Cindy arriving home. Once he heard the key in the lock, the front door closing and Vernon and Cindy exchanging good nights, Kenderson immediately dropped into an exhausted sleep.

SUNDAY MORNING

Sunday morning routines in the Kenderson household were hard to change. Maybe that was because Bandit began her vigil at the sliding back door at eight o'clock, and meowed until she actually had food in her mouth. She was impossible to ignore because, for a twenty-three year old animal, she still generated lots of noise.

As he lay in bed listening to Fran and Cindy's kitchen sounds, he felt like cussing. What a brilliant plan he'd devised for smoking out the killer. And who turns up but Pete with a cockamamie story about convincing Freddie to forget the circumstances of his mother's death. Whoever killed Hawkins apparently wasn't worried about Freddie and Ermon being in the house at the time of the crime, and he wondered why not. Would the boys have heard sounds? Probably not, the library door was sound proof. Wouldn't they have noticed a strange car parked in or near the Hawkins' mansion? Did that mean the murderer's car was in the garage? He wondered how many automobiles were parked in the Hawkins' garage. Pete lived under his father's roof, and so did Phil when he was in Santa Inglesia. Freddie had a Porche but he was grounded so often, the high priced vehicle was seldom seen on the streets. Earl Hawkins owned a limousine and used a chauffeur by the name of Red Calkins. Did the chauffeur have his own car? He snorted in disgust. He was going around in circles.

What if it was Phil Hawkins who'd killed his father? What was his motive to murder the man everyone said he admired. What if Phil was a Borderline Personality Disorder? If this was so, something happened to turn blind loyalty to murderous hate. If it was Phil, how did he get from the Elks Lodge to his home and back again to establish his alibi?

Sunday afternoon was often a hectic time at the Lodge. Family period was from one to six p.m. when parents brought their kids, who swarmed over the exercise apparatus in the gym and, as Kenderson knew from experience, loved diving and jumping in the lanes of lap swimmers.

Breakfast on Sundays had become a ritual. Bacon and eggs and toast, and forget cholesterol. Even the listening devices and tension didn't completely dampen the positive family atmosphere this morning. Kenderson half listened to the day's plans Vernon and Cindy had made with their friends. His mind was on Phil Hawkins, and he wanted very much to review his Diagnosis and Statistical Manual of Mental Disorders. He had only glanced briefly at the fourth version, which he'd purchased in 1995. With Medicare or insured private patients, a diagnosis was necessary. Probation wards seldom required Mental Disorder diagnoses.

Kenderson went to the den immediately after breakfast and pulled his DSM manual off the book shelf. On mid-page 650 he read that the number 301.83 was designated for Borderline Personality Disorders, and that all or parts of nine clinically observable criteria must be present to justify the BPD diagnoses. Summarized, the behaviors included "a pervasive pattern of instability in interpersonal relationships." Fear of abandonment produced unstable love/hate relationships including drug abuse, binging, suicide risks. The list of disorders went on. The description concluded with, "During their thirties and forties, the majority of individuals with this disorder attain greater stability in their relationships and vocational functioning."

Who could he talk to about Phil Hawkins' past? Fallon had provided one clue. The rage when frustrated. Could Nehi or Mary Washington have attended high school with Phil? Their ages were close. He phoned and when Lillian answered, he asked for her father. As usual, Kenderson realized he was not the caller she hoped was on the other end of the line. Remembering his phones were still bugged, he kept his message short when his friend answered. "Can I drive over now and talk to you and Mary?"

Fifteen minutes later he was sitting in the Washington front room, a cup of coffee in his hand. "So Mary, you were in the class behind Phil in high school. I know he was an outstanding athlete but what about his off the playing field behavior?"

Mary closed her eyes, struggling to remember details about her life fifteen years earlier. "He seemed like he was struggling to keep himself under control. Guys who played with him said he blew his top when things went wrong, and then he'd apologize all over the place afterward.

"Fallon, who played on the same team, told me that."

Most everyone remembers how hotly he defended his father. Once in class, some kid said Earl Hawkins was a racketeer and Phil came out of his seat and nearly choked the boy to death before he was pulled off. After that, none of the kids dared criticize Hawkins openly."

"What kind of student was he?"

"He acted bored, but he was very bright and graduated with honors."

"Where did he go to law school?"

"Santa Clara, I believe. That's where he met Nelson Ivers, who became the family's lawyer and I guess still is."

"Did he do drugs or alcohol?"

"Some, I guess. Everyone was into experimenting with drugs in those days." She paused in thought. "Seems like in his senior year, just before graduation, he told everybody he was going to drop out of school, but I guess his father put his foot down. I heard later, Phil did the same thing at Santa Clara."

Washington said, "What are you driving at?"

"If Phil Hawkins is a Borderline Personality Disorder, he could be the killer. Everyone says the two constituted a mutual admiration society. But with borderlines, if they feel betrayed by the person they idolize, the admiration can turn to hatred. Which brings me to the question: What was the so-called expansion plan anyway? Pete admitted Phil and his father quarreled over the issue, but what was it? Somehow, if I'm right, Earl Hawkins had to have demanded, even threatened, Phil to do something that ran deeply against the grain. Phil has a social conscience and Earl's demands may have threatened basic principles Phil believes in."

"So he has an alibi?" Washington said.

"Fallon told me nobody really checked out Phil's story. I'm going to the Elks Lodge this afternoon and ask about Phil's being there last Sunday afternoon."

"So what if people saw him?"

"Then I've got to figure out how he got from the Elks to the mansion, had time to kill his father, then get back without anyone noticing he was gone."

"A tall order."

"But possible. Sunday is family day and the place is overrun with kids. Someone could be gone for a short time and not be missed. Besides, there are a few outdoor courts for tennis and volley ball and a huge parking lot. Maybe he went outside."

"You're going to ask alibi questions at the Elks about our new state senator?"

"New, if elected."

"Unless Orin Silvester, his opponent, drops dead or Phil Hawkins is arrested, the Hawkins organization will keep on electing its candidates."

Kenderson rose and thanked them for the coffee and information. At the door, he said, "I'll keep you briefed."

The Washingtons wished him good luck and then he was driving back home, deep in thought about how to check on Phil without being too obvious. As he drove into his driveway, he'd already decided there was no subtle way to ask questions about Phil.

Fran was in the kitchen, her face questioning. He silently beckoned her to follow him to the patio. Once there, he told her what Mary Washington had told him. "What she described are symptoms of BPD. But the DSM cautions against jumping to conclusions. People with Mood Disorders have some of these same symptoms. The difference is that BPD is present from childhood on. Mood Disorders are often transitory. I may be jumping to conclusions but Phil's mother was supposedly an alcoholic. Phil was just a child when his father went to prison. His mother may have been so unstable as to create severe abandonment fears in the boy. If she were a borderline herself, the odds are that Phil would be one, too."

"So what's next? Fran asked.

"Check out Phil's alibi for last Sunday afternoon."

"At the Elks?"

Kenderson nodded. "How about coming along?"

Her forceful response was no surprise. "Anything to get out of here." She was near tears, "I feel so damn violated by those bastards. I'll do anything to end this nightmare."

With Vernon and Cindy gone, it was easier to fix sandwiches and eat at the patio table where they exchanged ideas about how to check Phil's alibi.

Kenderson said, "I'm curious why he dropped in on a Sunday afternoon. That's family day. You remember what a madhouse it was when we took our kids. Parents yelling, kids running and shouting. Total chaos! Why would he drop in to relax, as he said. He could have stopped at one of his exclusive clubs in Fresno."

"Then no one might have been able to verify his being there."

Kenderson brightened, "Right."

"Are you going swimming?"

"I'll take a suit. How about you?"

"Gym shorts and a walk on the treadmill."

SUNDAY AFTERNOON

At three thirty, they left for the Elks Lodge. Once there, Kenderson went to the indoor pool and Fran headed for the exercise room. He recognized one of the retired men who swam with him mornings at six. He greeted Jim Carruthers, who was keeping watch over his two grandchildren splashing in the shallow end of the swimming pool.

"You down here most Sundays?" Kenderson asked.

"Yes, the kids like it and my wife can use the exercise room while they're in here. Don't see you here on Sundays."

"Right, I was looking for Phil Hawkins. He said he comes down once in a while on Sunday afternoons."

Carruthers said, "I saw him come in last Sunday about four o'clock. He swam a few laps, then used the Jacuzzi. Don't think he's a regular, though."

Kenderson spirits sagged. He would be lucky if Carruthers could provide an answer to his next question. "Any idea when he left?"

"As a matter of fact I do. We walked out with Hawkins about five o'clock. We had to leave by then because it was my wife's turn to arrange refreshments for the retirees group that meets Sunday evenings at our church."

He thanked Carruthers and left to find Fran. Three strikes and you're out. Only he'd had about five strikes and nothing to show for it. He didn't feel like swimming and Fran, on hearing his news, said she'd had enough exertion for the day.

At home, Kenderson retrieved his notebook from the den and joined Fran on the patio. "As a sleuth, I'm becoming an expert in going up blind alleys. What am I failing to see?"

He looked at the list of suspects he'd written down earlier in the week and, one by one, went over the list with Fran.

Arnie Setich and Pete Hawkins' alibis were confirmed by a dozen or more customers at the bar they frequented. Now Phil Hawkins' time between four and six were accounted for. Frustrated, he thought about Freddie. Was the boy capable of deceiving him in a matter as serious as murder. That was part of the problem. Freddie was clearly happy his adoptive father was dead. At the gut level, Kenderson could not make himself believe Freddie had killed Earl Hawkins. Fran agreed with his assessment. She was silent for a few moments and then said, "Who says he died between four and six o'clock?"

"The medical examiner."

"But how do they determine the time of death?"

"A lot of different things. Castro told me the body cools at about one and one-half degrees per hour. Room temperature is a factor. So, the ME must have figured he'd only been dead about an hour or an hour and a half before the housekeeper discovered the body."

"Could he be wrong?"

"What do you mean wrong? That's his business to know how long someone's been dead."

"You said, room temperature effects how quickly a body cools?"

Robert White

"Yes, you're right. It seemed cool in the library. But that means the body would lose heat more rapidly. Outside, it was about ninety four or five degrees that day, as it's been all week."

"So a man like Hawkins can afford a first class air conditioner and a complex, programmable thermostat. If Phil had programmed the thermostat to heat the house, the body would cool much slower. Is that right?

Grinning, Kenderson rose and hugged his wife. "You may have something, hon." His brow furrowed.

"But Freddie was there. He and Ermon would have noticed a change to sudden heat. Or would they? If the boys were into ear-shattering rap or heavy metal, would they have even noticed the change in temperature?"

"Could Phil take that chance? He knew the housekeeper was off, but what about Freddie?"

Both were silent, beginning to have doubts about their analysis. Another dead end?

Kenderson began slowly, choosing each word with care. "While I was in the library, I noticed a thermostat on the wall. Could the library have a separate heating and cooling system? Could Phil have programmed the thermostat to introduce intense heat into the library, after killing his father, to retard the loss of body temperature? Could he have also programmed maximum cold just before he knew Mrs. Nabors, the housekeeper, would return and discover the body at six thirty?" Fran listened, nodding her head.

"He would want the temperature in the library to return to normal coolness. Couldn't he have programmed it so that the temperature, at the time of the discovery, wouldn't be questioned?"

Kenderson said, "That would be ideal. But could it be done that way?"

"Phil needed to buy himself at least a half-hour to cover his time. He may have done better than that."

They had the same thought at the same moment. Fran spoke first, "How can any of this be proved? It's a great theory but now what?"

Kenderson paused in thought. "There was a top grade computer on Hawkins' desk. If the temperature was controlled by that computer, the transaction might still be in the memory."

"Kind of a long shot, isn't it?"

"I can tell this to Fallon, but I'm not sure we'll need to. Phil is under a lot of stress. He may even be suicidal. He's looking for someone to talk to. I've sensed he wants very much to talk to me."

"All well and good," Fran said, "but I want to get this hypothetical sequence of events clear in my mind, okay?" Kenderson nodded. "Phil arrives at the mansion between three and three thirty. He's hired a rental because he's already decided to kill his father. He parks it on the next street. No time is wasted in an argument, nothing delays his picking up the trophy and braining his victim."

"He's wearing light gloves."

"He immediately programs the computer, as we said."

"So he arrives at the Elks at four, or even earlier, and his alibi is airtight."

They were both quiet, reflecting on Fran's analysis.

"Problem. This evidence is circumstantial. All Phil has to do is deny it's true."

"Right. Murdering your father is trauma enough, but he's also lost the person who's been the centerpiece of his life. His voice tells me he's beginning to feel depressed."

"So he still doesn't have to admit anything."

"Correct, but if he's emotionally adrift, he's feeling evil, deserving to be caught and punished. This is a symptom of BPD."

"You said people with this problem become more stable with age."

"Yes, but the basic problem is fear of abandonment and loss of love. He's just eliminated the one person he could count on to be there when needed. No matter how much he hated his father, because of what the man was forcing him to do, he desperately needed his emotional support. I believe Phil is looking for someone to take his father's place. I sense he'd like to tell me all about what happened."

Fran raised questioning eyebrows.

"I believe he would talk his head off. If I did invite him to confide in me, I would have to warn him up front that if tells me he committed a crime, I am duty bound to report it to the police."

"Very strange, very weird."

"He's a very sick and troubled guy."

"What now?"

"Get in touch with Al Fallon tomorrow. Tell him what we've come up with."

Robert White

SUNDAY EVENING

Weary of speculating, Kenderson proposed a dinner at Chevys Mexican Restaurant and Fran accepted. A Margarita helped reduce the tension, and the beef tacos, refried beans and rice made Kenderson want to go home and relax. Fran looked like she could join him. Just before driving out of the parking lot, the car phone rang. He exchanged puzzled glances with Fran before answering. Calls on the cellular usually meant trouble with their kids or those on Kenderson's caseload. He said hello and returned to his parking space, holding the phone for Fran to hear also.

"It's me. Phil. I need to talk to you." Kenderson knew he had to stop Phil from revealing anything important.

"Don't say any more, this line isn't secure. Where are you?"

"I'm parked across the street. I've been following you."

"Wave your hand out the window and I'll walk over and talk to you, okay?"

The answer was sluggish. "Okay, I'm waving."

Kenderson spotted a hand slowly moving from the drivers side of a blue sedan. He said to Fran, "That may be the rental car. I'll walk over and talk to him. Drive to a pay phone and tell Fallon what's happening. Tell him he may want to have a Deputy DA on hand if Phil decides to confess. And tell him

Phil, and the rest of us, could be in immediate danger if our conversation was overheard."

Fran nodded her understanding and drove quickly out of the parking lot. Kenderson hoped his analysis was correct. Otherwise, Phil might have decided the best solution was to have *him* join his dead father. Although it was nearly dark, Phil's face looked pale. Kenderson spoke first. "Do you want me to get in?"

Phil sounded hopeless when he said, "Please do."

Kenderson sensed he had to take the initiative before Phil sunk into an even deeper depression. "I'd like to hear what you have to say but as an officer of the court, if you tell me you've committed a crime, I must report it. Is that clear?"

Phil nodded. "I did it."

Phil began to ramble and Kenderson realized he was over his head, not knowing the legal ramifications of listening to a confession. He needed Fallon and a Deputy DA now to record Phil's statement. "Phil, before you say anything more, can I use your car phone to make a call?"

Silently, Phil handed him the phone. He quickly keyed in his own cellular number and after four rings, a breathless Fran answered. "Tell Fallon to meet me at the hospital where Vernon had his broken arm set. I'll give you this number." When he asked Phil for the digits of his portable, he had to repeat the request several times before Phil could recite them. Fran said she'd heard the numbers and would relay them.

Kenderson shut down the portable, then turned to Phil, who appeared even more depressed. The confession could wait. Phil needed medical attention at once. "Phil, is it okay if I drive your car. I think you should see a doctor right away."

Receiving a bleak nod, Kenderson exited the passenger side and, moving around the car, waited for Phil, who remained motionless, head down. He repeated his request several times before the assemblyman finally slid over. Getting behind the wheel, Kenderson knew one more question had to be asked. "Are you carrying a gun?"

Phil nodded.

"Please give it to me."

Slowly Phil reached behind his back and drew a black automatic from his belt. Kenderson held his breath, ready to wrest the weapon away. Phil almost deferentially reversed the weapon and handed it, butt first, to the social worker. Under the dash light, Kenderson checked to see if the safety was in the on position. It was.

"Is a shell in the firing chamber?"

Phil nodded. "You're sure. All I have to do is move the safety to off and the gun will fire?"

Kenderson took Phil's low grunt as affirmative. He carefully slid the automatic under his belt.

"You thought of using it on yourself?"

Phil slowly nodded. "I would have but I couldn't leave my dog, Jeff. Pete hates him and would ship him off to the pound."

Kenderson started the car and made a U turn, heading back to the freeway. Santa Inglesia's Kaiser Hospital was five miles south of Chevys. Phil remained silent while Kenderson reflected that Phil's actions and words confirmed his BPD diagnosis. As he drove, he felt a familiar twinge of fear, wondering if his call to Fran had been overheard. He'd made sure not to mention the hospital but Santa Inglesia had only four hospitals within the city limits. It might be only a matter of minutes before Setich and Simstead would discover where he was heading.

They must have been worried when Phil didn't answer his phone calls and stopped negotiating with Setich. Phil now constituted an even bigger threat than Freddie ever was. The assemblyman had inside information about the illicit organization's past and future plans. Full of remorse for killing his father, they would suspect he'd feel compelled to reveal the organization's inner secrets. Santa Inglesia and Oso County law enforcement and judicial system could not stop him from going to the Attorney General's office in Sacramento, where his word as the son of Earl Hawkins and an assemblyman would carry weight. Arnie Setich would have only one solution for that problem. Find Phil and kill him before he could talk.

Entering the south on-ramp, Kenderson stayed in the right hand lane and immediately began to scan the cars behind him. He looked for a dark Cadillac, and its lethal passengers. The glare of headlights behind made any detailed identification of oncoming cars impossible. He figured the car that got on his tail and stayed there would be Setich and his thugs. In a moment, a dark sedan was tailgating the Chevrolet rental.

His attention nervously focused on the rearview mirror, he was startled by the sudden appearance of another sedan coming up on his left. In the side view mirror, his eye caught a flash of the passenger raising what looked like the barrel of an automatic weapon. Setich was taking no chances on being outmaneuvered. Kenderson stomped on the gas pedal and found himself reaching for the gun. His mind suddenly whirled with irrelevant fears. If he fired the gun, would the Board of Behavioral Science revoke his License? Would the National Association of Social Workers Committee of Inquiry deem his shooting a gun on a freeway a violation of ethics? He recognized he wasn't thinking straight but as the car on his left drew into firing range, his survival instincts took over.

Crossing his right hand over the steering wheel, his thumb flipped the safety from on to off. He fired twice. Judging from the reaction, the first shot must have hit or grazed the driver because the sedan swerved into the left lane, and the automatic weapon bounced onto the pavement as the holder disappeared from sight. Kenderson was sure the second shot had been low. Maybe it had penetrated the door and hit the gunman.

He knew his troubles were far from over. Setich would be pulling alongside any second and start blasting. He moved to the faster lane and increased speed. The speedometer climbed to seventy then seventy five. He glanced at Phil, who was still bent over in the seat oblivious to the danger. The turnoff to Kaiser Hospital was still three miles ahead. No way was Setich going to let him or Phil reach a populated area. He guessed the automatic held at least eight or nine rounds, but the gun was no match for a rapid fire weapon. His desperation grew. Should he try to sideswipe the Cadillac? All the chase sequences he had seen on TV flashed in his mind. But he was no stunt driver capable of doing a one eighty in the middle of an intersection. Anything he tried could jeopardize the lives of the other drivers on the freeway. What he needed was help!

He thought he heard the wail of a siren behind him. He prayed fervently, let it be Fallon or Castro, not a fire truck. As the alarm grew louder, he saw the Cadillac pull out to his left and speed up. He wondered what the rental car would do flat out. He knew he was about to find out. Going back to the turnoff lane was no longer possible. It was going to be a race and he was sure the rental couldn't outrun the Cadillac. The wail grew louder. No fire truck was going to catch up with the racers. Please, God, let it be the good cops. He could see red lights flashing on the domes of two pursuing unmarked cars. They were closing in behind him and the Cadillac. He almost laughed. Saved because he was speeding. He'd take the traffic ticket, anytime.

He slowed and Fallon's face peered out of the passenger side of the nondescript sedan, beckoning to pull into the right hand emergency lane. One hundred feet ahead, the Cadillac had been pulled over and plain clothes detectives, guns drawn, surrounded the stopped vehicle. It was a relief to see Arnie Setich, the hulking Pete Hawkins, and Curt Simstead emerging with hands over their heads. He could imagine Setich sneering that the arrest was a farce and he'd be out within the hour.

Fallon was dropping a flare, directing traffic to move to the next lane. A moment later he was grinning at Kenderson, who suddenly became aware he was trembling, and thankful he didn't have to stand. He said, "What kept you? I thought we were goners."

"This Assemblyman Phillip Hawkins?"

Kenderson nodded and then a second man joined Fallon. "I'm Investigator Jake Flowers from the State Attorney General's office. Did Mr. Hawkins confess anything to you?"

Kenderson thought for a moment. Phil was on the verge of confessing to killing his father but he hadn't said so in so many words. "No, but....."

Agent Flowers jumped in. "Forget the *but*, we'll take over. Any objections?

"The man is suicidal. He needs medical attention. I was on my way to Kaiser Emergency..."

Again Flowers interrupted. "We'd like to talk to Assemblyman Hawkins right away. We think he's got a lot to tell us about the Hawkins organization. The Attorney General's Office has been interested in Oso County politics for many months now. So we'll take care of everything, okay?"

Flowers and another agent moved to the passenger side, opened the door and spoke to the recumbent man. "We'd like you to come with us."

Phil looked up, first at Flowers and then at Kenderson. Nodding toward Kenderson, he said, "This man understands me. I want to talk to him about something terrible that's happened."

"We won't worry about that now. We want you to tell us about your father's organization. Will you help us?"

Phil nodded, and assisted by Flowers, got out of the car and was solicitously helped into the rear seat of the sedan Fallon had come in. Kenderson was dimly aware that traffic slowed as it approached the flashing dome lights and parked cars in the emergency lane.

Fallon said, "Pretty good shooting for an amateur. Just talked to Castro. He's stopped the other car."

Kenderson felt his face grow numb. "Did I kill anybody?"

Fallon laughed, "No, but you scared hell out of the driver, and the guy who was going to make spaghetti out of you and Hawkins caught a spent slug in the belly. He'll live."

The relief made him want to sag down in the seat and stay there.

"Follow me. You've got to make a report on what happened."

"Let me call Fran, first."

Using Phil's phone, he dialed his own number and heard anxiety in Fran's voice. "I'm okay. The state has stepped in and has taken Phil Hawkins into custody. First priority is to get him to talk about his father's organization. I think he's ready to do that. You and the kids start looking for the bugs so we can get back to normal living again. Love you."

Fran said, "ditto" and then he was entering traffic behind Fallon's car. Glancing down, he saw the automatic on the seat beside him. His first thought was to toss it out of the car, but Fallon and the others already knew he'd used it. It was pure luck nobody had been killed by his wild shooting. For the moment, he wasn't ready to rejoice that he and Phil Hawkins were still alive thanks to his pulling the trigger.

At the police station, Phil was nowhere to be seen. Fallon said the state's boys had taken him to Fresno because they wanted privacy, and Setich and his crew were being processed at the Sheriff's office.

Under Fallon's guidance, Kenderson dictated a careful statement, covering only the attempted freeway assault on him and Phil Hawkins by Setich's enforcers. Whenever he mentioned Phil's involvement in his father's death, he was advised this was not the major question at this time. In the end, no statements were recorded as to who did or did not kill Earl Hawkins.

Kenderson had given Phil's gun to Fallon, requesting his role in the capture be eliminated. "It's okay by me," the cop said, "but the whole story's going to come out sooner or later."

"Later is better," Kenderson replied.

Before he signed his statement, Kenderson told Fallon his family were looking for bugs. "What if they don't find any? Can somebody from here go over our house with a detector?"

"No sweat. Just let me know and I'll send our guy along."

Kenderson was driven home by a patrolman, who insisted on complimenting him on the night's shooting. "It was righteous, man, they'd have killed the both of you."

Fran's look of frustration turned to joy when he walked in the front door. She flung her arms around him and started to cry. Vernon and Cindy crowded close. "The TV said you saved Assemblyman Hawkins, Dad. That's great."

Kenderson heard his voice sharpen, "Enough, already, shooting people isn't what social workers are supposed to do."

"But Dad....." Fran put a quieting arm on her son.

Robert White

"Honey, we looked under lamp shades and tables and the TV; we can't find any little buttons. Isn't that what the miniature microphones are supposed to look like?"

"Yes, that's what I've been told. Let's have one more sweep and if we find nothing, Fallon said he'd send a technician over tomorrow to check our house."

Different areas of the house were assigned, but after fifteen minutes, everyone returned to the front room empty handed. Fran spoke, "Who said the house was bugged?"

"I think it was Castro or Fallon who said the house *might* be bugged. They were wrong." Glancing at his watch, he said, "I propose we go to bed. This has been a long day for your Mom and me."

Later, as they lay in bed, Fran said, "The newscaster made no mention about who killed Earl Hawkins. What do you make of that?"

"When my statement was taken, the same thing happened. I was told *that* crime wasn't what the police were interested in now. I think the Attorney General's investigators are behind this. My guess is they want Phil to appear as a snow white witness when he reveals what he knows about the widespread corruption that's been going on in Oso county. I'm sure Phil will talk his head off, in part, to alleviate the awful guilt he's feeling now. Later, he may be charged with a lesser crime, or given the opportunity to plead self defense."

"So, our detective work went for nothing?"

"No, getting to Phil before he did something self destructive was important."

SUNDAY AFTERNOON, ONE WEEK LATER

The Washingtons and Al Fallon, who brought Sarah with him, were sitting outside on the patio. Glasses of cold beer went down easily on a warm Indian Summer day. Disappearing bowls of pretzels and potato chips kept Kenderson on his feet replenishing the drinks.

Fallon had the most news and he shared it with zest. "Who murdered Earl Hawkins is a taboo topic with the state guys, who are leaning on the local cops and the media. When we talked to Phil, he was willing to tell it all, including his programming the computer to slow down the body's temperature loss. Pretty good detecting, guys."

Fran grinned and took a bow but Kenderson didn't join her. Fran asked, "What about Setich, Pete Hawkins, Simstead and the rest of his thugs?"

"A newly formed grand jury is going to hear about a horrendous history of extortion and murder that goes back years. Phil Hawkins can't wait, according to Flowers, to get on the stand and spill his guts. He's evidently resented Setich's role with his father for a long time. The man is an ethical human being, who has urged improvements in education, campaign financing and other progressive reforms. He admits to turning his face away from the corruption he witnessed. The explosion happened, Flowers thinks, when Earl threatened him,"

"About what?" Washington asked.

"Phil isn't being asked a lot of direct questions pertaining to the murder, but Flowers thinks Earl Hawkins was pushing Phil, if elected state Senator, to promote extortion rackets in the new counties he would be representing. That apparently tore it for Phil. Like Jay said, he worshiped his old man in a sick kind of way but more than that, he needed the stability and structure his father provided. He threw it all out the window when he blew up."

Kenderson looked interested. "That would account for his rapid mood changes. He was a lost little kid, looking for someone to cling to. I believe he wanted to confide in me, have me become the stabilizing person in his life."

Mary was grinning when she chided Kenderson. "He'd have wanted a gun toting, shoot from the hip, social worker helping him?"

Everyone laughed and Kenderson joined in. People were not going to let him forget the freeway episode for a long time. Might just as well go with the flow, he decided.

Somebody mentioned Harold Fisher. Mary Washington said she'd seen an item about the man peddling his story to one of the tabloids.

Sarah, who'd earlier told the group that Phil had also revealed details about Hawkins' bilking of her father's fortune, said the family assets would be returned to her. Looking younger and prettier than he'd ever seen her, Kenderson wondered if she and Al Fallon were an item. She asked about Freddie.

"He's with the Converses. He's at the age now where he can control the medications himself. He may not need Ritalin or any other drug later on."

Robert White

"Did he change?" The question made Kenderson thoughtful for a moment before he said, "Both of us changed. I began to set some limits, and he began to see that all adults are not abusive or untrustworthy. I'll visit him for now every two weeks, and later, on a more extended basis."

"What about Reverend Nichols," Kenderson asked Fallon.

The detective grinned. "He's got an airtight alibi. Guess what it is?"

Kenderson laughed. "Other mens' wives get him in trouble and later out of trouble?" Fallon, chuckling, nodded.

"Understand you have an interview with Brad Miller of *California Now*? You going to do it?" Fran, smiling, was enjoying herself.

Kenderson smiled back. "Yes, I'll do it and you know why?"

A chorus of "No's" resulted.

Kenderson was grinning, as he said. "I told him I didn't want to get into trouble with the National Association of Social Workers or the Board of Behavioral Science with a lot of publicity about the shooting. The guy laughed, and asked me if the men shooting at me were clients?"

Everyone laughed again. "I told him of course not. He said, then you didn't do anything unethical did you? That's when I agreed to go for the interview."

Just then Vernon and Cindy, along with Lillian, came out of the house to announce they were hungry and where was the pizza? Kenderson rose and reached for his car keys. That was one thing he'd forgotten to do.

"I'll go, Dad," Vernon volunteered. With a sigh, he handed over the keys to the venerable Datsun. "Son, please drive carefully."